# RETURN
## OF THE
# MALPEDS

Trebor Tales, Book 2

CAROLINE C. BARNEY

*Relax. Read. Repeat.*

Return of the Malpeds (Trebor Tales, Book 2)
By Caroline C. Barney
Published by TouchPoint Press
Brookland, AR 72417
www.touchpointpress.com

ISBN-13: 978-1-952816-23-9

Editor: Jenn Haskin
Cover Design: Codex Art & Apparel

Map image design: Michael William Aldinger

Visit the author's website at carolinebarney.com

First Edition

Printed in the United States of America.

To my parents, Valerie and Richard,
who gave me the world.

# PROLOGUE

Dusk clung to the sky as darkness pulled at the corners of the horizon. The air was still, thick and smelled rancid. The white form of the stony giant lay in the field and the dark of the night that settled into the sky shrouded its body. The shape of the giant had crumbled into a pile of stone that now only held the smallest echo of the terror it had once caused. Coldness seeped into the field, engulfing the space with its bite.

Then, it appeared.

Tiny, slithering, silent.

Another joined it, oozing from the form of the dead giant.

They moved quickly, low to the ground, smooth and deliberate. From every hole, crack, and opening more appeared. Like water pushing its way out from an underground rapid, they sprang and flowed out of the dead giant. But they did not take the form of water, they did not reflect the sparkle of the moon as it rose in the sky, they were not fluid. They were dark and they skittered around, escaping from the hidden places that hung under the dead form of the giant.

Thousands of tiny, dark creatures flowed into the field, their presence consuming the space. A low hiss caught in the wind. The sound carried across the field mingling with the smell of death that seemed to run alongside it. They began to move, scrambling on top of each other, climbing, slithering, running. They moved across the opening, gaining speed as they scurried towards the dead tree trunk that stood at the corner of the field. They took over the trunk, climbing up its side, racing around it, again and again. Then, just as the sound of the hissing and the smell of rot became too much to bear, they slowly disappeared. One by one, they stole into the trunk, their shadows escaping into the hollowness of it. The field was silent once more. The dead giant in its pile of rubble now looked cold and lonely again, still and forgotten. Until suddenly its white surface reflected a red glare, bouncing color from its stony skin.

From the trunk, shooting from its top, a red mist sprung into the air. It hung in the sky over the field; the colored haze lifting to the sky. Fog rolled into the space and the red glow hung on it, seeping into the dusky air, taking over the field and everything in it.

And that was how it stayed for a long time…red and silent.

# CHAPTER 1

Stella inhaled deeply and grinned as the wind swept through her fur and the sun warmed her skin. The sky was so peaceful that her racing thoughts took flight on the wind and left her with a sense of calm and peace. No worries tugged at the edge of her mind for attention. The lush green that whirled below her added a fragrance to the air that smelled clean and fresh. She took a deep breath and filled her lungs, letting the cool air slide down her throat and fill her chest. Stella giggled as she pressed her face into the smooth feathers of the great bird, and let their silky touch tickle her nose.

It had been like this for two years, since her return from the terror of fighting the giant malped and finding her father. Every time she flew with the bird her mind felt free and clear. Each morning she rose with the sun before any other Trebor was even stirring. She scurried down the great tree's inner stairs and slid quietly out of the huge, arched doors at its base. She'd climb the outside of the great tree and happily feel the warmth of its bark and tingle of its leaves brush over her as she made her way to the very top of the tree.

There, she waited for the bird. It always came. She would sit in awe as the tiny dot on the horizon grew and slowly showed the silhouette of the bird. Its song greeted Stella before she could even see its bright red and yellow plumage. The gold tips of the bird's wings glinted in the sun as it drew close to her, and often she'd have to squint her eyes as the brightness of it was so bold. It never got old for Stella, the sound and sight of the great bird appearing before her, knowing it was there just for her. The joy of the bird landing before her, ready for her to climb aboard, was as great now as it was the first time she climbed onto its broad back. She never doubted it would come and always knew that her morning flight would be as rich and magnificent as all the days before.

This day was no exception. The vibrant green on the forest floor was only rivaled by the bluest of blues that ran along the riverbanks, and the brightest of yellows that reflected the sun on the drops of dew that ran along the thick brush's tangle of branches. Though nothing ever compared to the radiance of her home, the great tree. Each day, growth and light seeped from the tree into the lands of Bori. From its roots, it pushed healing into the earth. This was how it restored the land of Bori after the ravage of the storm.

Over the past years, Stella had watched as the tree's power radiated from its core, bringing life back to the soil and plants that surrounded it. In ripples of impact, the forest and crop fields had recovered beautifully and the Trebors were once again enjoying the fruits of the forest and earth. Stella lifted her head to look at the tree in the distance, it stood tall and strong, high above the forest lines as it reached into the clouds. She smiled as she thought more about how it never stopped giving to her tribe. Even when she had ventured away in the storm, the leaves and acorns from the tree had saved them. She patted her pocket to feel the leaves she had stuffed in it on her climb up the tree. She never went far from home without taking some of it with her. She was never going to make that mistake again.

The bird glided over the mubble hole. Stella loved how the water glinted in the sun and it reminded her of the lazy days she often spent with Snu and Fasha, her best friends, swimming and sunning on its shores. An array of colors jumped into her vision. She leaned further over the bird's shoulder to look more closely at the forest floor. *Yes! Yes! The evershi!*

# CHAPTER 2

Dotting the forest edge Stella spotted the shy bloom of the evershi flower. There were only a few, but their bright colors were not to be missed. The evershi flowers only make a brief appearance, but their arrival meant the growing season was ahead for the tribe. This meant there was celebrating to be done. Stella couldn't wait to get back to the other Trebors and tell them she had caught a glimpse of the flowers. News she knew would mean it was time for the Festival of the Evershi. Each year when the evershi flower made its quick appearance, all work stopped and the celebration was called to order.

The evershi flower had been the first thing to reemerge from the forest floor after the storm. Its rainbow of colors had filled the land of Bori and given the Trebors hope that they could recover from the terror. Now, when the flower is spotted, it is a reminder of all they have overcome and how the tree saved them. A reminder that means the biggest celebration of the year.

"Today's the day," she hollered into the air above her. A bubbly feeling caught in her chest and she laughed. She lay her face against the soft feathers of the bird and wind rushed across the fur on her cheeks. She didn't care where they flew, she knew it would be wonderful, she felt happy that she didn't need to decide, she just held onto the bird's wings and went wherever it chose, as visions of the evershi flowers soared in her mind. Soon though, the anticipation of telling the others about the evershi flowers got the best of her, and she called to the bird to head back home. She couldn't wait to tell the rest of the Trebors that the evershi was in bloom. But most of all, she couldn't wait to tell Ebert. He would be so happy for the celebration ahead and a break from the tribe's work. It was too bad he hadn't been with her this morning. He sometimes joined her, but he had not wanted to get out of bed this morning. In fact, it had been a while since he had flown with her. *Now he'll wish he had,* Stella thought.

The bird slowly descended to the treetop, its magnificent wings harnessing the wind to soar smoothly to its resting place. Stella slid from the bird's back and wrapped her arms around its neck; its bright feathers tickled her nose but felt warm against her fur. "Thank you," she whispered and stepped back for it to take flight. She waved as the wind's currents carried it away, sending it in circles in the air above her.

Quickly, Stella climbed down the tree. Her feet dropped into the clearing at the bottom of the tree and she skipped to the arched doorway at the foot of the tree. The door was now swung open and the happy sound of Trebor families starting their days greeted her as she stepped inside. Tiny Trebor children were running up and down the staircase in the middle of the tree; happy to find each other and start a new day. Mothers and fathers called to them to remember their lunches, mind their elders, and all sorts of other instructions for the day.

Stella smiled and barreled up the steps toward her home. She rushed her way up the steps swiftly, bouncing two steps at a time to move as quickly as she could. It was hard not to start yelling to everyone she passed, "The evershi are out," but she knew that a grander announcement needed to be made, and besides she wanted to tell her parents and Ebert first.

"Hey, watch it," Ebert growled. He was barrelling out of their home and bumped into Stella who was just about to step inside.

"Oh, sorry, morning," Stella panted as she spoke. "I have great news."

"I don't have time Stella, Yapa and Yama are already up and talking about work that needs to be done today. I've got to run to Elder Malc to get the elder assignments for the day so that they can get the crews organized." As he spoke, he pulled vigorously at the straps of his overalls to cinch them.

"But you can't believe what I saw…"

"Later. You'd better get in there, you're late today!" And with that, Ebert scampered down the stairs.

Stella shrugged her shoulders and walked into her home.

"Stella! Good morning my love," Yapa exclaimed, he pulled his daughter in for a hug. "How was your flight this morning?"

"It was amazing. I saw the first evershi flowers of the season at the forest's edge!"

"That's magnificent news," Yama said as she joined her husband and daughter. "I wonder if others have seen them yet, although it seems it's always you that sees these things," she said as she stroked the back of Stella's hair.

"I wish Ebert had been with me to see them. I tried to tell him, but he was in a hurry to get to Elder Malc."

Yapa sighed and shook his head. "That boy's in such a hurry to have the work done so he can hang out with his friends that he forgets to see what's around him. Such a hurry to be done that he misses these things along the way."

"That's a nice way to put it," Yama replied. She rolled her eyes. "He needs to understand that the work is important and not think of it as secondary."

"Oh, he's fine," Stella replied. "He gets his work done and he knows more than most how important sticking together and working hard is."

"You'd think so," Yama whispered. "Well, the evershi, this is marvelous news. We need to add festival preparations to the master schedule. Perhaps you can follow Ebert to Malc and let him know. And take Ebert his rumple fruit, he'll be hungry if he doesn't eat more."

Stella turned to leave, but Yapa grabbed her hand, his eyes glistened as he spoke, "Nothing brings me more joy than how committed you are to your morning flights, and the fact that you spotted the evershi first is such a gift, enjoy sharing the news with the others."

Stella rested her head on her father's chest and he folded her in his arms for a hug. "Thank you, Yapa. I love you," she said. He smiled at her and she skipped away and out to find Elder Malc and Ebert.

# CHAPTER 3

Stella stopped abruptly on the landing outside her home. Everything was strangely quiet. Up and down the tree's core a hush settled around her. She looked around to see why everyone was so quiet, but couldn't see anything out of the ordinary. She quickly descended the steps, but couldn't help noticing that the other Trebors were diverting their eyes as she passed them. She couldn't tell if they were actually busy or just trying to look away. There was now a low mummer of voices, but Stella decided she was being paranoid and must have simply not noticed the noise before, as she was very preoccupied with the evershi after all.

She stepped out of the tree and just outside the entrance she spotted Ebert and his friend Rufo. Ebert's body was stiff and he flayed his arms around. Stella glanced at the other Trebors who were clearly listening to what Ebert and Rufo were saying, but once again, they turned their attention away. Stella walked past them quickly towards Ebert.

"Ebert, everything okay?" she yelled over to him as she walked closer.

Rufo glanced at Stella and suddenly strode away, his broad shoulder brushed against her as he rushed off.

"What's that about?" she asked when she reached her brother.

"Nothing, we were just talking about some of the work that needs to get done today," Ebert replied.

"Huh, but why was everyone listening to you both?" she asked. "And did you notice it was quiet for a while and no one seems to be making eye contact?"

Ebert shrugged his shoulder and smiled at his sister, "Rufo was cracking jokes, everyone was listening because he's loud and funny."

"That's true. He's loud. But the other Trebors were…"

"Stel, stop worrying. I've got to get to Malc," Ebert interrupted. "Did you already see Yama and Yapa?"

Stella rubbed her temple to stop the quick flash of pain she felt. She focused on her brother. He smiled. The noise of the other Trebors picked up again and Stella shrugged off the strange interaction. There was too much excitement in the day to let a small thing with Ebert stop her happiness.

"I'm coming with you to Elder Malc," she replied.

"Why?" Ebert asked.

"This is what I was trying to tell you before, I saw the evershi in the forest today."

"By the mubble hole?" Ebert asked and then quickly gave his head a slight shake.

"How'd you know that?" Stella asked.

"Oh … ah … I had no idea … was just guessing … did I get it right?"

Stella nodded yes. Her nose twitched.

"Ha! What a lucky guess!"

"Yes–lucky," Stella replied. She looked carefully at her brother and his eyes wrinkled at the corners as he smiled at her.

"Hopefully we'll get to work on the festival preparations today, and not be assigned to anything else," Ebert said. He looped his arm through his sister's, and they headed around the tree to look for Elder Malc. Stella quickly forgot what was bothering her. It was such a beautiful day that the rest of the Trebors were already outside and beginning the day's activities. It seemed there was nothing but fun ahead in the day. She caught sight of Snu with a crowd of friends and dragged Ebert to see him.

"Evershi in the forest," she announced as she got closer to the group.

The group turned to look at Stella and Ebert, Snu's eyes quickly darted from Stella to Ebert and back before he replied, "Festival time!" The others in the group patted Stella on the back and all exclaimed their happiness that this meant days of rest and celebration to come.

"We're on our way to tell Elder Malc," Stella told Snu. "Any interest in coming?"

"How could I resist?" he replied. He did not look at Ebert as he spoke, only directing his attention to Stella.

Together, the three walked toward the waterspouts at the back of the tree where Elder Malc usually began his rounds for the day. It was still a remarkable sight to see the number of new roots the tree had pushed through the forest floor around its base. They climbed up and over the smooth, dark bark that popped through the mossy soil.

"I had another one of my dreams last night," Ebert offered as they walked.

"Was the giant malped in it?" Stella asked.

"Yeah … it was the same as usual … it had its scaly hands wrapped around my body and I couldn't breathe. The strange thing was that this time his whole body glowed red. It wasn't just those red eyes, but all of him. I woke up before anything else happened, but it was a creepy change."

"Maybe the dream is trying to tell you something," Snu replied. Stella glared at Snu, it frustrated her when Snu was not more sensitive to Ebert. For the past year, Snu seemed to disregard Ebert's feelings. Stella couldn't understand why he was wasn't more concerned about Ebert's dreams. Stella and Snu were fourteen now, five years older than Ebert, they might have moved on from their terrifying time with the giant malped, but Ebert was still working on it, he was much younger.

"I bet it was just the red of the malped's eyes made you dream of it all in red," Stella tried.

"No … it was different…" Ebert's nose twitched quickly and the fur on the back of his neck quivered. He reached back and smoothed it with his hand, shaking his head.

Stella put her hand on her brother's back and gave it a single pat. "Next time come with me on the bird, I bet it would help," she said. "I go to bed thinking about the morning with the bird and it makes me sleep so much better. Remember, it worked for you when you were coming with me?"

"Yeah … maybe," Ebert mumbled, but he wasn't paying any attention to Stella anymore. He was staring at Rufo who was standing next to Elder Malc. Snu noticed Rufo and Malc and stopped walking to watch the two speak.

"Let's give them a minute," Snu suggested.

"No, come on, we've got to get the day going," Ebert replied and rushed ahead towards Rufo and Elder Malc.

"Morning Malc," Ebert interrupted as he got closer. Elder Malc looked up and regarded Ebert with a puzzled expression. His eyes followed Ebert carefully as Ebert approached. Stella looked from one to the other and wondered when Ebert had started to call Elder Malc, Malc.

"Good morning Ebert. Are you here for your parents? I have the crew work all laid out for the day, let me get it for you to take to them." He eyed Ebert carefully before rummaging through his satchel for his writing notebook. As he pulled it out, he noticed that Stella and Snu had come along as well.

"Ah Stella, Snu, wonderful to see you this morning. What word have you for me? For I presume that is why you have come along with Ebert on his simple errand."

"The evershi are out!" Stella exclaimed.

"Praise be! It's remarkably early this year!" Elder Malc said. "But early or not, that means time for celebration. You are sure my child?"

Stella nodded eagerly.

"All right then. Snu, why don't you climb to the tree's top and blow the signal horn. Everyone must hear the news." Snu took off climbing towards the upper branches of the tree and Elder Malc turned to Stella.

"Where did you see the flowers?"

"By the forest's edge, near the mubble hole," Stella replied.

"Hmmm … Rufo was about to tell me something about the mubble hole," Elder Malc looked around to find Rufo, but he had left. "Ah well, I suppose he'll find me later."

"Elder Malc, we would love to lead the preparations for the festival, if you think we are ready," Stella said and smiled at Elder Malc's kind face.

Elder Malc studied Stella's face closely and then turned to watch Snu climbing up the tree. Snu's body became smaller and smaller as he got closer to the top. Elder Malc then closed his eyes, turned his face to the sun and stood there silently. Stella looked at Ebert carefully, who rolled his eyes and shrugged his shoulders. She grinned back at her brother, but quickly pulled her lips together and returned her focus to Elder Malc. He opened his eyes and again looked at her.

"So be it," he said. "You and Snu will run the festival this year. I can see that you are filled with gratitude towards our tree and that each day you watch out for the needs of the other Trebors, it is time you have a larger role." He pulled Stella into a hug and squeezed her tightly for a brief moment.

Stella quickly brushed away the tears that formed at the side of her eyes, her pride over being assigned the task was brimming over.

"Spectacular!" Ebert exclaimed and rubbed his hands together.

Elder Malc patted Stella on the back while turning his attention to Ebert.

"You will help with the waterspouts today, and here are the notes for your parents," he said to Ebert.

Ebert kicked at the ground and stared at Elder Malc. Elder Malc did not move, just kept his sight leveled on Ebert. Ebert kicked once more and threw up his arms. He grabbed the pages of notes and stormed away.

"Ebert, Ebert…" Stella yelled after him and took a step to follow. Elder Malc gently placed his hand on her forearm.

"Leave him, he has to learn for himself," he said.

Stella's face burned and she tried to force a smile. She wanted to run after her brother, tell him to apologize, and ask him to behave better, but Elder Malc's hand remained on her arm and she knew better than to disregard him.

"Can't he just help Snu and me?" she asked shyly.

"No," he replied and pulled his hand from Stella's arm just as the signal horn blasted its low noise into the sky above them.

All at once, Trebors appeared from everywhere, emerging from their homes inside the tree, swinging out of the tree branches, running from the forest. The open, flat clearing that surrounded the tree was instantly full. The buzz of curious voices filled the space. The excitement made Stella's heart beat faster. She could hardly wait for Elder Malc to tell everyone why they had gathered. Elder Malc and Stella made their way through the growing crowd to the center of the clearing.

At the center, a huge, circular stump served as a platform for announcements. The rings in the stump circled in the hundreds, making it very wide. It had also been smoothed so that it was very flat and an easy place to stand on to be seen and heard. This central spot in the clearing was an important part of the tribe's life. Elder Malc climbed onto the tree stump. He lifted his chin slightly and looked over the crowd with a grin pulling at the edge of his mouth. Not too far from where he stood, Snu jumped from the tree, his job with the horn done, and walked towards Stella. Elder Malc waited until Snu was near-by and the crowd was silent.

"Fellow Trebors," Elder Malc began. "It is with great joy that I share that the evershi have been seen!"

Whoops and hollers filled the air. Snu bumped his shoulder against Stella's and she laughed. Elder Malc held his hand up for silence.

"Celebrations will begin after two sunsets," he continued.

Again, he was interrupted by the spontaneous shouts of excitement from the growing crowd. He held up his hand.

"The Festival of the Evershi is a special time for our tribe. We remember again how the great tree, our home, saved us and helped us bring back to life the lands of Bori. The evershi shows its face so briefly, a flash, to remind us of hope. For this, we are grateful, and must have the most joyous of celebrations."

Someone from the crowd yelled, "Who will run the festival this year?"

"I have asked Stella and Snu to oversee the festival," Elder Malc began, but the thunderous applause drowned out anything further he could say. Instead, he let out a deep laugh and smiled at his fellow Trebors.

Snu grabbed Stella's hand and shoved it into the air. The two held their clasped hands high above their heads. Everyone clapped harder. A few of the smaller Trebors ran to them and threw their arms around them. They giggled as their little hands grasped Stella's fur. All at once, Snu and Stella were swept off their feet by a group of other Trebors and carried above the crowd, surfing from one set of hands to the other. They rolled across the top of the crowd like a wave and were placed on the stump next to Elder Malc.

Stella's face burned and she looked around to see if she could spot Yama and Yapa. She pushed her hair from her face and tugged at the corner of her shirt. Snu laughed beside her, waving to everyone gathered around. It felt like the clapping and applause lasted forever. Eventually, the crowd grew quiet and Snu and Elder Malc turned to Stella. They both beamed at her. She froze. Her eyes wandered over the now quiet crowd. She was speechless. Then she saw Yapa standing in the middle of the crowd. Yama stood next to him with her hand resting on his arm. The white streak of fur on Yapa's fur that ran along his chest up to his neck made him stand out and she was glad for it. Yama placed her hand right on the white streak in his fur, a streak that only Stella and Yapa had, and then she locked eyes with Stella. Yama nodded and smiled. Stella felt her confidence come back. Like her Yama and Yapa she too could do bold things.

"Thank you Elder Malc. Thank you everyone!" Stella shouted. "I'm so thankful that the bird flew where I could see the evershi today; so glad that I can share the news with you all. Let the preparations begin," she yelled. She threw both hands in the air and clapped them over her head.

Song instantly filled the clearing. A small breeze blew into the space around them and the sound of the song swirled through the air and swept-up into the sky. Tears streamed down Stella's cheeks as she looked into the faces of her fellow Trebors. Their wide eyes glistened and showed the joy they all felt and it was contagious. Snu drew a deep breath and began to sing with gusto. Stella listened for a few moments as she waited for the catch in her voice to go away. And then, she too joined the singing,

*Flowers appear on the earth,*
*The season of singing has come,*
*The song of peace is heard in our land,*
*The evershi, the evershi*

# CHAPTER 4

"What's he doing?" Stella whispered. Sweat dripped down her forehead and pooled on the ground in front of her. It left a muddy ring by her feet. She was on all four peering through the brush in front of her and trying to keep from making noise in the dry leaves that lay all over.

"Shhh, just watch," Snu whispered back.

Stella and Snu had been crouching in the brush next to the mubble hole for almost an hour. Stella's knees hurt and she was annoyed by Snu's insistence that they stay quiet. The announcement of the evershi had been such a thrill, but Ebert had been nowhere to be seen. The rest of the day had been a blur of festival planning and Stella had fallen into bed and slept through dinner and right up until sunrise the next day. She had no idea what Ebert had been up to; she just assumed he was working. Snu had thought overwise. And so now, she found herself hidden amongst the scratchy branches wondering what her brother was actually up to.

They watched as Ebert paced back and forth at the edge of the mubble hole. His fur stood on end and looked crazy as it pointed in all directions at once. He muttered to himself and only stopped occasionally to stare into the forest that surrounded him. Each time he stopped, Stella and Snu held their breath until he began his pacing again.

"I know he's upset that he's not helping us prepare for the festival, but why'd he be all the way out here on his own?" Stella wondered.

"I don't know, but he was here before sunset yesterday as well," Snu replied. "After we finished our planning yesterday, I came out here to see the evershi for myself and that's when I saw Ebert. He was doing the same thing then. Pacing and muttering."

Stella wanted to crawl out from her hiding place and confront her brother, ask him why he was out here all alone and why he wasn't working on the waterspouts. Something kept her clinging to the brush though. She sat up slowly, resting on the back of her heels.

"Let's go," she said. "Nothing has changed for an hour; I can't sit here anymore." Snu nodded.

Slowly, they backed out of their nook, careful to be as quiet as possible. Each leaf that rustled and branch that cracked under their crawling knees sounded enormous to Stella. Fortunately, the birds and animals that filled the air with their determined tweets, scratching ,and scurrying masked Stella and Snu's noises and they were able to slip away undetected. Once they were far down the path on their way back to the tree, Stella finally broke the silence.

"I'm worried about him. He hasn't come with me to fly with the bird in months and his dreams are more frequent. He was so little when we saw and experienced all that we did after the great storm, maybe it was too much, maybe he needs something else," Stella said.

Snu did not reply. Stella stopped in her tracks, stood in front of Snu, and raised an eyebrow.

"What?" She demanded.

"Come on Stella, we can't blame everything on that," he replied.

"You make it sound like he's done something wrong," she hissed. "It's my fault, not his, that we all ended up terrorized by the giant malped. We all know that."

"It wasn't your fault then and it's not your fault now that he's acting so weird."

"It was. If I hadn't been so busy trying to do it all myself, he would have never been in that situation. You know it ... and so do I."

"HE is the one who followed you, remember?"

"But I should've never left the tree and the tribe in the first place."

"It wasn't just you Stel, I was there too."

"Only because you had no choice."

"Come on, let's not do this again. It is past us now. We're safe. We all need to move on. You don't have to defend Ebert all the time, he has to take responsibility for his own stuff too."

"But the dreams, he can't help those."

"Maybe not, but he's in charge of how he copes. That's not up to you."

"I'm his sister," Stella sighed. "Who else is it up to?"

"You really don't see it do you?"

"What ... see what?"

"How everyone else looks at Ebert? How half his stories don't make sense? How he always has a smile for you, but others get his rage?"

Stella took a step back from Snu and glared at him. Snu

crossed his arms and said nothing back. She tried to reply but her whole body shook with anger. Snu uncrossed his arms and reached a hand out to Stella. She slapped it away, turned abruptly, and ran. She was so furious she could barely see straight. Snu just didn't understand. He didn't have the same blood running in his veins as Stella and Ebert.

"Stel, you can't just run away from me and what I'm trying to tell you," Snu yelled after her.

Stella stopped and turned to look at Snu. She pointed her finger at him, extending her claw dramatically. "You think I'm running away? Ha! You don't know me the way I thought you did. I just can't stand listening to you talk anymore that's all. I'm not running away from anything other than you!"

And with that, she broke into a sprint, leaving Snu standing alone in the woods. Snu yelled after her, but she ignored his calls and just kept running. Tears ran hot down her face as she ran, and she darted off the path and into the heavier brush. The scratchy branches grabbed at her as she ran, but she didn't slow down. She threw her arms back and forth in front of her, breaking through the thickness of the forest to forge a path. She was numb to the chorus of noises in the forest as the blood pumped so loudly in her ears she could hear nothing else. She ran and ran and ran until she had no breath left and collapsed in a heap on the mossy forest floor. A great sob escaped her lips.

*Why did Snu have to be so cruel? Did she really not understand her brother?* Something inside told her there was more to what Snu had to say, something she ought to pay attention to, but she couldn't think how. She was Ebert's sister, his biggest fan, his protector, if something else was going on with him she would know. She flopped onto her back and looked at the canopy of branches and leaves above her. Birds jumped from branch to branch. The blue sky above peered through the thicket over her head.

As she laid there, a fog slowly rolled into the sky and settled in the air surrounding her. It turned grayer and grayer until the forest around her grew shrouded and eerie. A cold swept into the air and Stella shivered. The fog grew denser and left huge drops of water along the branches above her. More cold air blew into the space around her and the fierceness of the sudden freezing air grabbed the drops of water and turned them into ice. More quickly than her eyes could even keep track of, each drip of water rolled along the branches and dripped off into growing icicles.

Spears of ice grew long and pointy as the water turned to solid. They shimmered as they spread, growing longer and longer with each passing moment. They were beautiful, forming sharp points that sparkled. They grew so rapidly that Stella rubbed her eyes to be certain they weren't playing tricks on her. She was mesmerized by them. Time stood still and Stella gazed at the structures that dangled above her. The fog now enveloped her so completely that she could barely see anything but the glint of the icicles.

Something rustled in a pile of leaves nearby. Stella broke her gaze and jumped to her feet. She strained her eyes to see through the thick, gray fog. Ebert's head popped up from a bed of leaves not too far from Stella. His blond hair stood to attention and his fur was covered in debris. It looked like he had been asleep on the forest floor. Despite the fog, she could see that his eyes were glassy and he stared into the distance.

"Ebert?" Stella said.

He did not reply, but instead just stared ahead into the murky space around them. She was sure it was him and yelled for him again. He remained still, not responding to her calls. Stella watched him quietly for a few moments before yelling again. No reply. Just as she picked up her foot to move towards him, she heard a crack, it was a long, slow sound that echoed around her. She glanced around carefully but saw nothing. *Craaaaaack.* The noise grew louder. Stella looked up, and to her horror, saw that a long, zig, zagged split was forming in the largest of the icicles. *Craaaaaack.* She looked around wildly as she realized the cracking icicle was directly over Ebert. The icicle cracked again, a small drip of frozen water hit Ebert's face and slid down his cheek. He did not move. *Craaaaaack.*

"Ebert wake up! MOVE!" Stella screamed.

She was frozen. Her legs wouldn't move. She tried to rush forward, to get to Ebert, but nothing happened. She attempted to scream, to warn him, but her open mouth made no noise. She tried again and only a croak slipped out.

*Craaaaaaack.* The split in the icicle grew.

Stella's heart beat so quickly that she could barely breathe, and yet her body still would not do anything. Again, she tried to run. Again she tried to scream. Nothing. All she could do was watch as fear gripped her. The split in the icicle made its way to the top. It snapped. The icicle dropped from the branch and spiraled through the air towards Ebert. Faster it spun, faster, but Stella's voice could not break free. She stood helpless, stuck heavy on her feet, robbed of any means to help. The sword flew. No words could stop it.

# CHAPTER 5

"WATCH—"

Finally Stella's voice broke free.

"EBERT, EBERT," she screamed again.

Slowly, methodically, Ebert turned his head and looked at Stella. His eyes burned into hers. She screamed.

Ebert's eyes glowed red.

The icicle was now only a few feet from hitting him.

"Move, move," she yelled hysterically.

Her legs suddenly sprang into action.

She jumped towards Ebert.

*Darkness.*

The warmth suddenly hit her face. Brightness glared into her vision. She blinked and shook her head.

Sunshine.

Green leaves.

*No fog.*

*What? Where am I? What happened?* Stella thought and sat up quickly. *Where's Ebert?* She was sitting on the forest floor and scrambled to her feet. She whirled around, but there was no sign of Ebert. The fog was no longer there, it was warm and the sun was shining. It was as if the fog had never been there.

Stella dropped slowly to the ground as reality set in. She had been dreamed. Her head spun as her body tried to catch-up with what her mind knew. Relief flooded her. There were no icicles. Ebert was fine. He wasn't even there. She reached to touch the back of her head where leaves clung to her hair and fur. She carefully pulled them out one by one and looked around her. It had felt so real and her heart still raced as if it had happened. She couldn't shake the uneasy feeling.

As she sat there waiting for her heart to slow back down, she began to feel foolish for having made such a scene with Snu. Sitting in the sun, pulling leaves from her fur, relief tingling her fingers and toes, she found she no longer had the same angry feelings for Snu. She rubbed her eyes to clear the fog and anxiety, and peered up at the sun above her. The sky was still crystal clear, and the birds in the trees hadn't skipped a beat. It was time to push all this worry out of her mind and focus on the festival.

Stella rubbed her face to get rid of the tight feeling from the salty tears that had dried on her skin. She had no idea how long she had been asleep. She shook off the uneasy feeling that still crept through her and forced a new, single-minded focus into her mind, Ebert would be fine, whatever was going on, she could help him fix it and everything would be back to normal. She hoped this thought would settle into her bones instead of the dread that inhabited them. She pulled the rest of the leaves out of her hair and brushed the moss from her fur. With determined steps, she started to retrace her route back to the path.

After a short while, Stella made her way through the brush to the path and quickly turned back towards home. As she walked, not too far away, she spotted Snu. He was sitting on a tree branch that hung low and parallel to the forest floor at the edge of the path. She stopped to watch him when she realized he hadn't seen her yet. He swung his short, stubby legs back and forth while he whistled the tune of the evershi song. He was busy with his hands, stringing together a chain of flowers.

One by one he connected evershi flower after evershi flower. They made such a long chain that it looped over the branch and dangled onto the forest floor below. She was amazed by the number of colors he had found and how much progress he had made putting them all together. The flowers on the chain blurred together into a beautiful waterfall of colors. But what drew Stella's attention the most was how peaceful Snu looked while he worked.

He was in no hurry, he was just *happy*, all tangled up in a mess of flowers. He was steady and focused like nothing else mattered. The million things that they needed to do before the festival began after sunset and sunrise seemed to be nowhere on his mind.

Stella quietly approached him. She purposely made a few small sounds so that she didn't scare him by suddenly appearing out of nowhere. She was careful though not to be too noisy as she didn't want to intrude on his peace. Snu looked up and when he saw Stella he grinned slightly before looking back down and continuing to build his chain. Stella climbed up onto the branch next to Snu and ran her fingers along the flowers. They sat like that for a while. Quiet and still.

"Sorry," Stella finally said. Snu nodded his head once and kept working. Apology accepted.

"I don't know why I get like that about Ebert, I know you were trying to help and I just got crazy," she continued. "But I'm better now. I have a plan. Whatever's going on, I know I can fix it with him."

Snu stopped and turned to Stella, his eyes were soft and they smiled for him. "Okay," was all he said in reply.

Stella pursed her lips and shrugged her shoulders. It didn't feel like he meant *okay*, but she didn't want to argue again. They sat quietly together for a few minutes before she spoke again, "What are you doing that for?"

"I was waiting for you," he replied. Stella felt an ashamed wave roll over her.

"And while I was waiting," he continued. "I saw an unusual number of evershi flowers growing along the path and figured I'd do something for the festival–ta da!"

He picked up the flower chain and swept it over Stella's head and onto her shoulders. She realized just how long she must have been asleep based on the great length of the chain. Stella smirked and rubbed her hand along the delicate flowers. They may only last for a few days, but while they were around, they really were spectacular. The chain hung around her neck and the sudden smell of the flowers so close to her nose made her sneeze. Snu laughed and looped another section of the chain around her neck again. Stella giggled and then sneezed again and again and again. The awkward noise from her nose made the two of them burst into fits of hysterics. Stella had to grab onto the branch with her claws to keep herself from falling off. It felt wonderful to laugh so freely after her scary dream, and this made the hysteria even harder to stop. Snu roared along, caught-up in Stella's crazy laughter. After a while, their laughter slowly stopped and they pulled themselves together and jumped from the branch.

"Look at the sun, it's far past center sky, and we've got so much to do still," Stella said.

She removed the chain from her neck and tossed it back to Snu. They had to get back to the festival preparations. Snu meticulously raveled the chain around his thumb and his elbow, careful not to let any of the flowers get caught against his claws. He took the fully looped flower chain and put it over Stella's head again. Drenched in the sweet scent of the evershi, she felt happy and threaded her arm through Snu's.

"Let's go," she said.

Snu turned to his friend and grinned. "Come on, I bet I get there before you," he teased, and off he raced down the path towards the tree.

Stella followed. The evershi chain swung wildly against her face as she ran, it blocked her vision as it bounced up and down. The sight made Snu roar with laugher which only made Stella cackle with amusement too. They barreled down the path, laughing and panting, both trying to be the first to reach the tree. As they stumbled into the clearing, they stopped short to catch their breath and get ready to jump back into the festival preparations. The other Trebors were all so busy bustling around, taking care of the usual work for the day, as well as preparing for the festival, that they didn't even notice the two giggling as they returned. Stella pulled the chain off and held it carefully draped across her arms. Yapa was the first to spot them.

"There you are my love," he yelled from across the clearing. "Where have you two been? It's not like you to miss the overseeing of everything. All okay?"

Stella diverted her eyes and mumbled a quick response, "Sorry Yapa … we just got caught up looking for some evershi flowers in the forest. Look what Snu put together."

Stella held up the chain of flowers for Yapa to see. Yapa nodded slowly but focused on Stella's face. He was not convinced. Stella hated not being fully truthful with Yapa, but didn't know quite what else to say, and certainly wasn't going to tell him about Ebert's strange behavior right then. She had that under control. So, instead, she threw her arms around his neck, gave him a hard squeeze, and bounced away.

From over her shoulder, she said, "Snu, I'll check on the decorations. Can you check on the feast?"

"Alright," Snu replied and also turned quickly to walk away.

As Stella scampered away, Yapa yelled after her, "Here if you need anything!"

## CHAPTER 6

The decorations for the festival were breathtaking. Stella had spent the rest of the day turning their simple clearing into a magical expanse. It was fit for the most impressive Festival of the Evershi they had ever had. At some point during the day, Fasha found Stella dangling precariously on the edge of tree branch trying to string up some flowers and realized her friend needed more help. She jumped right in and since that moment, they had been locked at the hip, leaving no detail untouched.

A busy crew of Trebors had been assigned to help Stella, and they had each been tremendously effective bringing Stella's vision to life. She was so grateful for their hard work and how they made her plan a reality. They all stood back from their effort and let the excitement of how well it had all come together wash over them. Giddy with pride and excitement, Stella tossed her arm around Fasha.

"Thank you," she whispered to her friend.

Fasha rested her head on Stella's shoulder and smiled. "You are most welcome," she replied. "It's really even more amazing than I imagined."

She was right, the clearing was alive with color and smelt

heavenly. In the center of the clearing, the huge stump Stella had stood on just days before with Elder Malc and Snu, was now transformed by a carpet of evershi flowers. They covered the stump completely, draping over its edges and spilling onto the ground around it. The flowers swirled around the stump and flowed out into the clearing. It looked like a skirt twirling around, making the clearing appear as if it was about to spin into motion. More evershi flowers were knit together into a long rope that attached to the end of the flowers on the stump and then wove in a spiral around and around the clearing.

The flowers spiraled in a way that made a single, circular path from the stump to the edges of the clearing. Outside of the flower roping, tables and stools were set-up to fill in the space with plenty of room for everyone to relax and feast. In the middle of each table, a long twig from the great tree stood tall and pointed to the sky. The twigs glowed with the telling iridescent green of the tree and reflected the late day sun from their bark. The light they cast into the clearing was both bright and warm, and Stella's heart jumped as she took in the sight. She was sure this alone would bring such joy to her fellow Trebors.

And yet, the most spectacular part of the decorations was what they had done with the evershi chain Snu had linked together. Coming out of the stump in the center of the clearing, stood another much bigger piece of wood from the tree, although unlike the twigs on the tables, this one had been taken from the inside of the tree, so its bark was not rough, but smooth and warm. It was a tall pole reaching high above the clearing.

Snu's evershi chain had been broken into three pieces and attached to the top of the branch. They were so long that they flowed down from the top of the pole and ran all the way to the outer parts of the spiral rope of flowers. Except that with the evening breeze picking up, they now danced freely in the air above the clearing. They skipped on the wind, up and down, back and forth, as if dancing to a song that only they could hear.

Stella turned to Fasha and whispered, "It really is amazing isn't it?"

"I don't think the festival has ever looked like this before—I love it," Fasha replied.

"Thank you again for all of your help Fasha, I couldn't have done it without you."

"I'm happy to Stel, and besides we had to make up for your slow start this morning."

"Sorry about that, I got caught up helping Ebert with something," Stella answered.

"Ebert? I haven't seen him all day. Is he okay? He hasn't seemed himself lately."

"I think he's just tired, he hasn't been sleeping much, those nightmares are back."

"You think that's it? I haven't wanted to say anything, but Trebors are talking about him and Rufo and some big fight they had."

"I don't know what he and Rufo could be fighting about, they have been close since they were tiny Trebors," Stella replied.

"I guess they were yelling at each other, saying things like, it's too late now…"

"What's too late?"

"I have no idea … that's just what people heard them say when they were arguing. Do you know what it could be?"

"Maybe they were arguing about it being too late to change Elder Malc's decision to not let Ebert be part of the festival preparations?"

"From what I heard, this fight happened before that Stel," Fasha said carefully.

"Oh," Stella replied. "Did this argument happen the morning I saw the evershi?"

"Yes–I think so."

"I saw them together, maybe they had fought as it seemed to end quickly. I guess now that you mention it, I haven't seen Ebert and Rufo together since then."

"Probably nothing," Fasha replied. "Just wanted you to know what other Trebors were saying."

Stella smiled at her friend and was about to reply when she heard Yama's voice.

"Stella … come now … everything is done for the night … it's time for dinner," Yama yelled from the other side of the clearing.

Stella hugged her friend and skipped over to her mother, careful not to disrupt any of the decorations. Yama put her arm around Stella and led her towards the tree's opening. They laughed as they walked, both tired from the day's busy work, but excited for the day off and the celebrations that would follow after nightfall. When they got to their home, Yapa and Ebert were sitting at the table, they too were laughing. They both stood when they saw Stella and Yama and reached for their hands. They stood in a circle holding hands and smiling at each other. This was a ritual they had started when they were reunited after the great storm. They never let a day go by when they didn't hold hands and have this moment, remembering how lucky they are to be together. While holding hands, they always sing the same simple song of thanksgiving:

*We stand together, grateful and full,*
*We stand together, in warmth and light,*
*We stand together, no matter the darkness,*
*With home in our hearts, we stand together!*

Aside from her flights with the bird, this was Stella's most favorite part of the day. It was a great comfort to be with her family and know that they were just as glad to be with her. She had once almost lost them and now each day with them felt precious.

# CHAPTER 7

"Fasha?" Stella was taken aback to find her friend sitting on one of the tree's top branches waiting for her.

"Sorry to surprise you like this, but I was so so so hoping I could fly with you on the bird today?" Fasha exclaimed.

"You don't need to ask Fasha. You can always come. The bird isn't just mine. But why today all of a sudden?" Stella asked.

"I don't know, it just seemed like a good day to go with you. And I was thinking how happy you always are doing your chores and I wondered if it is because you start your day with the bird. So, I'm here to try! I just want the work to feel less boring."

Stella nodded her head but wondered why she'd never noticed her friend being annoyed or bored of the work. *What else haven't I noticed?* she thought. But, before she could ask Fasha anything more, the bird appeared and quickly lowered itself to pick up the girls.

In no time at all, they were squealing with delight as they soared into the sky. The decorations in the clearing were even more impressive from the sky. The colors of the evershi flowers blurred together and the dew that rested on their petals made them shimmer as they flew over them. The chains of flowers still blew slowly in the wind, as if waving to them from the ground below.

"Helllooooooo," Fasha yelled down to the flowers. Stella laughed harder and gripped the bird's feathers tighter so she didn't slide off. Just as well, because the bird took a sudden turn and Stella had to quickly grab onto Fasha's shirt to keep her from falling off. And of course, *this* only made the girls roar harder. As they sailed through the sky, happy and carefree, life on the forest floor below them was so vivid and alive that they soon fell into a stunned silence by the magnificence of it all.

They soared over the crop fields, where the rumple fruit grew in abundance on rows of bushes, and pink beans bounce on their vines waiting to be harvested. The kasha fields, the Trebors staple grain, were not yet in their growing season, but tiny buds dotted the fields, first sprigs ready to reach for the sun.

The quinolds, which take the longest to fully grow, in shades of red, purple, green, and brown, usually dip from the ends of the quinold trees. Although, in their early growth they only hung off the ends of the branches. Soon though, they would grow heavier and heavier until their enormous weight and length stretched to touch the ground. And only then, would they be ready to slice and eat. Stella's stomach growled as she peered into the fields and she wished she had eaten more the night before. Shortly, they veered away from the fields and followed the wind's currents to the denser forest area.

The girls gasped at the sight below them. In just a day, the evershi flowers had taken over the forest floor. They carpeted almost every corner.

"I've never seen so many evershi in one place," Fasha yelled to Stella.

"And I've never seen them so bright before," Stella replied. She cupped her hand over her eyes to look more closely at the remarkable sight below. They flew on, constantly in awe of all that sped past. As they drew closer to the mubble hole, they noticed something darting from its sunny edges into the canopy of the forest. It was quick and sent a glare of light that made both girls shut their eyes quickly.

"Did you see that?" Stella asked.

"Something moved over there. Right?" Fasha asked. She carefully opened her eyes and pointed to the far corner of the mubble hole. Leaves in a bramble of bushes shivered slightly and then just as suddenly as the movement started, it stopped.

Stella whispered in the bird's ear to do another loop over the mubble hole. As it did, the girls clung tightly to the bird's feathers and peered over its head to try and get a better look. There was another movement below.

"There." Fasha pointed to the bushes bristling on the forest floor.

"I saw it too," Stella replied. "What was it?"

They leaned over the bird's shoulders, but there was nothing further to see. Whatever they had glimpsed a sight of was no longer moving. Everything was quiet. The water in the mubble hole was smooth as glass. The shoreline buzzed with activity from the forest birds, but nothing jumped out to startle them again.

"It was too small to be a Trebor right? Or could it have been someone holding something shiny?" Fasha wondered out loud.

"Can't have been a Trebor, that glare was too strange, and we know they're all at home in the tree, we're the first ones up." Stella shivered and the fur on her forearm shook. Fasha reached out and smoothed it back down for her. Stella smiled at Fasha, but had to work to shake off another chill that ran down her spine.

# CHAPTER 8

Back at the tree, Stella and Fasha saw Snu first and were delighted when he greeted them by bursting into song, *"Flowers appear on the earth, the season of singing has come!"* The girls grinned at Snu as he danced in a dramatic circle around them. But he cut the song cut short when they realized Elder Malc was walking towards them.

"Children, I am so proud of you," Elder Malc called as he got closer. "I feel that this will be the best festival the Trebors have ever had!"

Stella smiled broadly. Snu swept his hand into the air and made fists for cheering.

"Can we begin?" Stella asked.

"Indeed," Elder Malc replied. "Here children, stand with me on this gorgeous center and watch what happens."

From all of the openings in the tree, Trebors poured out and crossed into the clearing. They wore tunics of many colors, and rings of flowers in their hair. The youngest of the Trebors tripped over each other as they hurried to be as close as they could to the celebrations. Their parents followed closely behind, arms linked together as they walked, their bodies swaying happily. The sound of cheerful voices filled the clearing and the vibrant colors of the Trebors' outfits reflected the colors of the flowers as everyone joined in a circle around the spiral path of flowers. Another blast came from the horn, and now the elders walked towards the clearing, one by one, through the crowd of Trebors and into the swirl of flowers.

Yama and Yapa each waved to Stella and Snu as they took their places with the other elders in the rings of the flowers. They faced the outside of the clearing looking at the crowd of Trebors that screamed with delight. Yama waved her arms high over her head and Yapa and the other elders quickly followed to do the same. Soon all of the Trebors had their arms held high above their heads waving them back and forth, swaying from foot to foot. The sight was spectacular and the whole space buzzed with energy and joy.

A third signal was trumpeted from the horn and the crowd fell silent. Elder Malc climbed onto the stump covered in the blanket of flowers. He stood next to the tall pole that reached into the sky with its evershi chains flapping in the breeze.

"My good Trebors, today is a day of rest, today is a day of celebration," Elder Malc bellowed. The Trebors once again broke into a chorus of cheers. Elder Malc put up his hand for more silence.

"Today, we remember. Today, we do not forget the great storm. Today, we say thank you. We were kept safe by our great tree," he continued. Trebors continued to holler and clap. "And we wave our hands to the sky knowing there shall never be a storm like that again. The quick and abundant arrival of the evershi reminds us to pause and be grateful. And now … let the music and dancing begin!"

Stella and Snu quickly wrangled the ends of the evershi chains that were attached to the branch and handed them to the Trebors that came forward. Fasha giggled as Stella handed one to her, she was delighted for the dance to begin. Then Stella and Snu each grabbed a chain in their hands and lofted them above their heads. With one arm reaching to the sky and one on their hips they all bowed.

Music filled the air instantly and with great grace and beauty they began to walk in a circle around the pole, the evershi chains winding around it. They turned and unwound the chains, this time skipping. They stopped in place and danced with the chains above their heads, waving them like ribbons in the sky, they wove in and out of each other braiding the evershi chains against the pole in the middle, and then they turned and did the reverse, slowly freeing the chains and returning them to blow in the wind. Again, and again they danced around the pole, singing as they did, watching the petals fly free from the chains and fall throughout the clearing.

Stella felt breathless and her cheeks hurt from the grin she could not stop. As she spun, she saw Yama and Yapa singing. She saw Ebert with Rufo who also smiled and sang. She felt her heart jump and danced on. They danced until all the petals had been freed from the chains and then slowly one by one, they released the green strings left behind to once again blow freely in the wind.

Now the music became louder and faster and the Trebors all clasped hands. In a thread of Trebors, they skipped through the rings of flowers, adding new friends at every turn. Soon they were all dancing and singing together, one long Trebor chain, in perfect harmony. The chimes that led the music played louder, ringing brightly. They skipped and danced around and around in the spiral of flowers. The youngest Trebors joined in by climbing on their parent's backs and shoulders. They reached for the green strings blowing above them and laughed as the strings danced out of their grip. Elder Malc jumped from the stump where he had made his speech and grabbed Stella's hand.

She smiled as they switched directions and led the chain of Trebors around the great tree. Together they wove, hand in hand, around the tree. They raised their hands up and waved them with hands clasped together. The tree seemed to glow even brighter than earlier. The bottom of Stella's feet tingled as she danced close to the mighty tree's roots. For what felt like forever and not long enough, the dancing continued, until soon they all collapsed at the tables and stools in the clearing.

The feast that sat before them was full of abundance. Piles of yaza fruit were peeled and ready to eat. Pink beans hopped on the plates, fresh from the vines in the fields. Bread and pies lined the tables, and all the seasonings of the forest made the food more favorable than ever. As is tradition, the elders gathered around the stump in the clearing and raised glasses of rumple juice. Yama made the celebratory call to eat, "May the food fill your stomach, the juice refresh your body, and the time with each other feed your heart!"

"Hear, hear," everyone cheered and quickly dug into the food before them.

# CHAPTER 9

"Yapa have you seen Ebert?" Stella asked.

Yapa shook his head and patted Stella's shoulder, "Not since the dancing," he replied.

Stella shook her head and wandered away, slowly walking around the clearing looking for Ebert. She had caught his eye when they were dancing and he looked happy. He was even dancing with Rufo, which made her feel good. She was sure whatever had been bothering him must have passed and wanted to talk with him about the festival. She wanted to hear what he thought of everything.

"Stella, over here," Fasha called. Nearby, Fasha, Snu and a group of other Trebors their age all squeezed around a table piled high with food.

"Come sit with us, we'll make room," Snu added.

Stella jogged over to the table and her friends cheered as she sat down to join them. She realized she hadn't really eaten much since lunch the day before and dug in to some cooked quinold. She chewed slowly letting the sweet taste fill her mouth. Her body relaxed as she ate. All her duties were now complete, she had nothing but time to rest and eat. Now that the celebration dancing and traditions were done, they were all free of work and obligations. They could sing, dance, eat, sleep or whatever they chose for the day ahead. It was a time to be away from worry, and Stella was ready to relax more than ever. Snu smiled at her while she ate, he too was glad to have a break.

"Fasha was just telling us all about the evershi in the forest," Snu said.

Stella nodded, food still in her mouth.

"I was telling them how many there were and how they'd glowed even brighter than normal," Fasha added.

"Were they really throughout the whole forest?" another friend asked.

"As far as we could see," Fasha exclaimed. "Although, they were most dense near the mubble hole, right Stel?"

Stella listened and occasionally responded, but mostly she let the sun warm her fur and the food fill her belly. She was staring into the forest, listening to Fasha talk, when a quick rustle in the brush caught her eye. She quickly shut her eyes when a sharp light bounced off the leaves, just like she had seen in the morning. No one else at the table noticed. She stood up and walked towards the brush.

"What are you doing?" Snu asked. He following her quickly.

"I saw something at the forest's edge, a strange glare, I think I might've seen the same thing when we were with the bird this morning," she explained.

"I think you're probably tired from all of the preparations. Come on, come back and relax with the rest of us," Snu replied.

Stella pursed her lips together and slowly scanned the forest. There was nothing to see. She carefully swiveled to look along the other parts of the forest, but again, saw nothing.

"You saw nothing?" Stella asked Snu.

"Nothing," he replied.

Stella shrugged and headed back to their friends. She didn't last long though, as much as she wanted to sit still and relax, the sight in the forest unsettled her. Ebert popped back into her mind. She stood up.

"Where are you going?" Fasha asked.

"To look for Ebert," Stella responded.

"Come on … leave him to himself … enjoy your day," Fasha tried. But Stella shook her head "no" and Fasha knew better than to argue further. Snu instantly stood up and joined Stella.

Once they were out of earshot of the others, they stopped and Snu whispered to Stella, "My guess is that he is back at the mubble hole." Stella nodded; she had been thinking the same.

The two headed down the forest path towards the mubble hole. They walked in silence but Snu kept shaking his right hand and Stella felt a strange tingle run down her spine.

"I can't get the pins and needles out of my claws," Snu finally said. "I can't tell if I'm cold or if I'm just tired from all of the dancing and holding my hands up for so long."

"Probably both," Stella replied. She had the same feeling but was trying to push the strangeness out of her mind. She rubbed the back of her neck; a pain shot over her eye and she moved her hand to press her palm against her eyebrow. The pain lessened. Snu rubbed the fur on his chest and shook his hands again. As they approached the mubble hole they slowed their steps and tread carefully not to make too much noise. Eventually, they crouched down and climbed towards the brush at the corner of the mubble hole.

That's when they saw them.

Stella gasped and Snu grabbed his chest.

"This can't be!" Stella whispered. Snu did not reply, he just clutched his chest and groaned.

Stella turned her attention back to the mubble hole. There, standing next to Ebert, was a malped. There was no mistaking its giant, round head and bulging eyes, the pitter patter of feet running up and down its long, scaly body. Everything in her body screamed; except her voice. She had to save Ebert. But, the expression on Ebert's face kept her rooted in place.

That's when they saw it—Snu grabbed hold of Stella's hand—malpeds were everywhere. All along the shore the malpeds' feet made a rhythmic noise that echoed in their ears. As if dripping from the trees, malpeds dangled along branches and up and down the trunks. The air smelled like old burnt logs and rotten fruit all mixed together. Snu sneezed and the sound startled Stella back into the moment. Snu slapped his hand over his nose and they ducked further into the forest. The sat still, barely breathing for a few minutes. It seemed Ebert hadn't heard. They crept back toward the opening. They hadn't been imagining it. The malpeds were still there; thick in numbers.

"Ebert, check out what this one can do," Rufo yelled.

Stella swung her head to see Rufo high in a tree overlooking the mubble hole. They hadn't noticed he was there. He was sitting on a branch a thousand feet above them, a malped sat next to him. Without making another sound, Rufo jumped and a moment later the malped jumped after him. Snu gasped and jumped out of their hiding place. He ran as fast as he was able towards the place where Rufo was falling. He could see that Rufo was not going to make it into the water, his course was heading straight towards the ground.

"Do something!" Stella screamed. She also jumped from the brush.

Ebert's mouth dropped open as he watched Snu and Stella hurtle themselves towards Rufo.

"Ebert, do something!" Stella yelled again.

They weren't going to make it to Rufo in time. Tiny malpeds leaped from the trees and landed on the ground all around them, the sound of the pitter patter feet was deafening. Just as Rufo was about to hit the ground, the malped that jumped with him let out a piercing sound. As the sound penetrated the air, the skin under the malped's front arms stretched to form a thin, flat film. From under its arms, all along its long body, its skin stretched and ballooned out. Its whole body turned flat and wind rushed to fill the filmy skin. Rufo reached up and grab the malped's front arms, and like a parachute, more air rushed into the thin skin and caught hold of the air around them. Slowly now, Rufo descended to the ground. Swaying side to side as the air ballooned the thin skin of the malped, Rufo safely landed on the ground.

Snu stopped in his tracks and stared. Stella did the same. Rufo climbed out from underneath the malped. He and Ebert looked at each other. All around them, malpeds scurried into the forest edges, leaving the four alone, staring at each other.

# CHAPTER 10

"I—Ebert—what—" Stella stumbled over her words, unable to make them gather into a sentence.

"I can explain," Ebert said as he grabbed his sister's hand. "They are good Stella, they are good. They are not the same malpeds. These ones come from another mountain, lands and lands away from here. They have special powers. They can do amazing things!"

"This is crazy! Why didn't you tell us there are more malpeds!" Snu yelled.

"We were going to, but it's the festival, and we're just having fun with them," Rufo answered.

Snu didn't look at Rufo, just stared at Ebert. Ebert dropped Stella's hand and threw-up his own hands.

"This is why we didn't tell you. I knew you wouldn't believe me that they are safe to be with," Ebert said.

"How can you possibly think they're safe? Don't you remember what happened? Don't you remember how all of the small malpeds morphed into the evil giant malped? Don't you remember that the little ones were part of the big one all along? Don't you remember how we all almost died?" Stella screamed. Her voice was hysterical.

"Calm down. They're fine. They are from a different place, like Rufo said. They are harmless." Ebert replied. "They're good Stel. They just wanna play. They just wanna make us happy too. Harmless. You have to see. You have to try to understand."

"Ebert, show them," Rufo interjected. "It's the only way they'll understand."

Ebert nodded his head and walked to the edge of the forest. He called out to the malpeds, "Come back," he yelled. A red flash of light glinted from the forest and then one by one malpeds appeared. Their feet moved quickly and they glided into the space in front of Ebert. There were hundreds of them. Ebert turned back to face Stella and Snu.

Once again, the fur on Stella's neck rose on end and a dull ache settled behind her eye. Snu's breathing became heavier and so she moved closer to him.

"Did you see what that one did with Rufo?" Ebert asked.

Snu shrugged and shook his head in disbelief. Stella did nothing.

Ebert continued, "Well, each of them has a different thing they can do, each one has an experience for you that's totally unique. It's incredible. I'm seeing and doing things I've never done before. I feel happy when I'm with them. I feel like the nightmares that follow me are no longer there. I can be without my nightmare's haunting presence for a time when I'm with these malpeds."

Stella's shoulders sagged and she sat down; she was suddenly exhausted. Snu slid down next to her.

"How can this be?" Stella asked. Snu shook his head in response and Ebert hurried to be with them.

"Do you understand Stel?" Ebert asked.

Before Stella could reply, Rufo interrupted, "Watch," he said.

Rufo pointed to one of the malpeds and it quickly moved next to him. He put one foot on the malpeds back, but rather than flattening the small creature, it made the malped jump up and hover over the ground. Rufo put his second foot behind his first, in a row along the malpeds long, long spine. The malped and Rufo began charging towards the water in the mubble hole. They bounced as they hit the water and then skimmed across its surface. All around the water Rufo surfed, riding on the malped's back. A spray of water sprung from underneath them and scattered all around as they flew across the water. Rufo laughed and its sound echoed around the mubble hole.

"You see?" Ebert said. He searched his sister's face for a reply. Seeing none, he started running towards the water.

Stella jumped to her feet and yelled, "No!" But it was too late, Ebert throttled himself towards the deep water that Rufo was skimming across. He was waist-high before she yelled again, "You can't swim, what are you doing!"

And then out of nowhere one of the malpeds leaped onto Ebert's back and pulled him from the water. Up it pulled him, higher, higher. It could fly. Ebert spread his arms wide and whistled as he glided above them in the air. His body flapped underneath the tiny malped. It was impossible to understand how the malped could hold Ebert's weight.

"Just because it's fun Ebert, doesn't mean this is okay, doesn't mean you're safe," Stella screamed into the air above her. But Ebert couldn't hear, or didn't want to hear. He just soared higher and higher.

"We have to go back and tell the elders," Snu said to Stella. This sentence Ebert and Rufo had no problem hearing.

And from each of their places, one standing on water and the other dangling in the air, they yelled, "NO!"

Stella felt cold air on her neck and slowly turned her head to find a malped standing on her shoulder. She hadn't even felt it climb on her. Before she could swat it away or jump to her feet, it rubbed the top of its head along her cheek. The sensation was cool and comforting. The spikes that lined the frame of the malped's face were surprisingly soft. It cocked its head and pushed its eyes inches from Stella's. She tried to look into its eyes, but before she could focus, Snu grabbed the back of the malped and threw it from her. It skidded on the ground next to them, circled into a ball, and froze. Stella shivered and looked at Snu. He shook his head and she nodded hers. They had to put an end to this.

# CHAPTER 11

"I'm not sure we're doing the right thing," Snu said to Stella. They were sitting at one of the festival tables, smiling at each Trebor that walked by, accepting thanks for their hard work.

"He said they'd send them away and never go back to find them," Stella said quietly. Her eyes darting from one Trebor to the other. She hoped no one could hear them.

"Do you think he'll do it?" Snu asked.

"It's so dangerous. He must know that. I think we made it clear."

"I'm not so sure. You saw all of the things those malpeds can do, I even thought about staying and trying some of the tricks," Snu replied.

"Me too," Stella admitted.

"You did?"

"I don't know Snu, do you think Ebert could be right? That they could be from another place? Maybe they don't have anything to do with the evil we battled," Stella wondered.

"We saw the giant malped die, right in front of us. So, I don't think they could be from the same place. But that doesn't mean we ignore the danger," Snu replied.

"They look exactly the same," Stella said.

"Yeah … it's not right, Stel. We did the correct thing. Nothing good can come from all of this," Snu said as he pointed into the forest towards the mubble hole.

"He'll do it. He'll make them leave," Stella added.

"I hope so."

"He will. He always does the right thing when I talk to him, you'll see,"

"I don't think that's actually true Stel, there's something I've been wanting to tell you about—" Snu began, but he stopped abruptly when Elder Malc and Yapa appeared to talk to them.

"This day was a true day of joy for all Trebors," Elder Malc said. He patted Snu on the back and smiled at Stella.

"Thank you," Stella replied.

"You don't sound as excited as I thought you would after such a great success. Such an amazing day," Yapa said.

"Oh, sorry, I guess I'm just tired," Stella replied. "You're right, it has been an amazing day."

"Are you okay? You don't seem yourself," Yapa replied.

"I'm fine, everything's fine," Stella stumbled. "Well, it's just that, well, Ebert is—" Snu squeezed Stella's knee under the table and she stopped.

"With Rufo and on his way, we are waiting for them," Snu interjected.

"Alright," Yapa replied slowly, drawing out the last syllable and locking eyes with Stella. Stella looked away.

"Well, before they get here, we were hoping to ask you something," Yapa said. He did not let his eyes leave Stella's.

"Ah yes," Elder Malc jumped in. "Many of the Trebors were puzzled by the abundance of evershi flowers this year. It seems there are more flowers than ever before. How did you find so many? Did you travel further into the forest than usual to find more?"

"Or were the flowers you harvested in new locations? Did you notice anything different?" Yapa added.

Stella's throat tightened and the fur on her forehead instantly prickled with heat. She stammered out a quick response, "It was an unusually wonderful growing season for the evershi—I'm so thankful!"

Yapa and Elder Malc laughed.

"Leave it to the children to remind us to be thankful for what we were given and not to go looking for worry," Elder Malc said to Yapa. Yapa looked at Stella and creased his eyes, his nose twitched. In response, Stella hugged her father and said, "I will see you back at home Yapa. Once Ebert is back, we'll find you and Yama."

Yapa leaned back from his daughter and looked into her eyes again. Stella smiled and so Yapa nodded and turned to leave with Elder Malc. They walked away slowly and spoke in hushed tones to one another.

"Are you okay? You don't look right all of a sudden," Snu said.

Stella's heart raced and she looked around wildly to make sure no one was listening to them.

"Why did you cover for Ebert? Why didn't you let me tell Yapa?" Stella asked.

"I don't know … I guess I wasn't ready to give up on

him yet ... I guess I'm hoping he'll do the right thing himself before we have to involve the others. But really ... are you alright? You're sweating."

"What were you going to tell me before they came over?" Stella blurted out.

"Oh, ah, just that, Fasha told me that some of the Trebors think that Ebert and Rufo saw the evershi before you did, but didn't tell us all. Seemed strange."

"Oh no–oh no! It can't be. No. No." Stella whirled around quickly, frantically looking in every direction.

"What?" Snu asked. "My point was that I'm not sure he always tells you everything and listens to all you say."

Stella did not hear Snu.

"How could I not have seen it," Stella hissed.

"What? Stel, you are scaring me. What's wrong?"

Snu reached out to Stella, but she jumped back and shook. She was suddenly wild with worry.

"Breathe," he tried. "Come on, take a breath, look at me."

Hot with anger and confusion, Stella leaped away from Snu and started running as quickly as she could into the forest.

"Stella, stop!" Snu yelled.

# CHAPTER 12

The tangles of the brush caught in her fur as she pushed her way through to the forest path. Once on the path, she picked up her pace and sprinted as fast as she could. Her legs turned numb as she ran, but she pushed on, faster, faster.

"How can this be," she panted as she ran.

Snu huffed; his stride mirroring Stella's a few feet behind her.

"Stop," he tried again.

Stella tripped in a hole in the path. She flew forward and skidded on her elbow. Her fur ripped away from the skin. Snu stopped short and tried to help her up. She shoved his hand away roughly and jumped to her feet. She whirled back to look at Snu. Tears clung to her eyes. "I have to see, it can't be," she muttered.

"What?" Snu replied. Stella shook her head and began to run again.

The mubble hole soon came into focus before them. This time they did not hide in the brush, but pushed to the shoreline. Stella stopped short at the water's edge. Snu barely stopped in time before knocking into her. The space in front of them was empty. No Ebert, no Rufo, no malpeds.

Stella took off again. She ran to the far end of the mubble hole. Her steps slowed from the mud that clung to her feet. Snu grabbed her arm.

"Enough!" he yelled. Stella struggled free and ran a few more feet away. She dropped to her knees and dug in the dirt. She scraped and pulled with her claws until she yanked out a long root. She held it up to look at it closely. Snu just watched, his forehead wrinkled with confusion.

"Look Snu, look!" she hollered.

She shook it harder and dirt flung from the long multi-color root.

"Don't you see?"

Snu looked more closely and tried to see what she did.

"Don't you see? It is not normal Snu!!!" Stella yelled again. Tears streamed down her cheeks and she shook with emotion.

"I don't understand," Snu implored. "Isn't this the spot where you saw the first evershi while you were flying with the bird? Why are you uprooting them?"

"Yes! This is the very place I saw them first," Stella managed in between sobs. "One day I saw a small patch of evershi right here, and the next day the forest floor was covered. In one day, they spread everywhere. I just thought we were lucky, that it was a perfect evershi year."

"Okay… so they grew and spread faster than usual. What's that have to do with this root? Why are you so upset?"

"How do you still not get it?" she yelled. "Look closer!"

Stella pointed to the tip of the evershi root. The root had

the usual swirl of color; its tip was a vibrant red and then each of the colors of the rainbow merged in rings as the root grew thicker and denser. Snu shrugged his shoulder. He could see nothing different about the root. Then he blinked. His eyes stunned by a red glow that shot out from the tip of the root. Like tiny lightning bolts, red lines zig-zagged from the root as Stella shook it in front of Snu. It was the same red glare they had seen along the forest edge when they saw Ebert with the malpeds. Stella saw some recognition on Snu's face and sat back onto her heel and let the root fall into her lap.

"These evershi didn't grow normally. It wasn't just luck that they were early this year, or that they were so abundant, it was the malpeds," Stella whispered. She was spent.

"You think they had something to do with the evershi?" Snu asked.

"It's not the malpeds I'm worried about. It's Ebert. Ebert—" Stella said between great gasps. "He did this, I know it."

Stella could no longer control herself. Every part of her body shook. Pain shot up her neck and her eyes blurred.

"He did this," she said again.

Snu put his arm around Stella's shoulder and pulled her close to him. She lay her head on his chest and tried to take a deep breath. Instead, she ended up coughing loudly and sat up quickly to gulp for air. She threw her head between her knees and took small, shallow breaths. She closed her eyes and tried to pull herself together. Finally, she felt ready to say the words she was so afraid of.

"It was Ebert who made the evershi grow like this, he

must have asked the malpeds. It all clicked when you said he and Rufo had seen the evershi before me, right after Yapa asked if we noticed anything different this year."

"I don't understand," Snu tried.

"He cheated. Don't you get it? He cheated. It wasn't the beautiful miracle of the first flowers we were celebrating. It wasn't real. Somehow Ebert had the malpeds control the growing. I know it. I feel it. None of this is right," Stella swept her arms towards the thick tangle of evershi flowers. "It's ALL WRONG! And now—" Stella began to cry again. "And now, I know it's not just the malpeds that aren't good, Ebert isn't either. He lied to us. He lied to me. He's never lied like this."

"You think he asked the malpeds to make the evershi grow?" Snu asked. He was still confused by what Stella was saying, and very concerned about helping her.

"He must have figured out what the malpeds can do and used them to make the evershi grow," Stella tried again. "It's the only way to make sense of all of it."

Full recognition now slid down Snu's face.

"He didn't want to work, he wanted the festival time, so he had the malpeds help him," he said.

"He lied. These malpeds made him lie. How could he want their tricks and unnatural ways more than us?" Stella asked.

Snu put an arm around her shoulders without answering.

"Oh Snu," Stella cried. "What are we gonna do?"

"Stella?" It was Ebert. Out of nowhere, he stood right in front of Stella. "What are you doing?"

Stella jumped to her feet and shoved the root in front of

Ebert's face.

"Did you do this? Tell me. Did you? I want the truth!"

"Why are you so upset? Calm down. Everything's okay," Ebert replied.

"It's not okay, Ebert. You did something to the evershi. Somehow you made them grow. I know you. I can see it."

"I didn't do anything wrong!"

"Yes, you did. This is not natural," Stella yelled. She shook the root hard again.

Ebert took a step back from his sister. His eyes bore into her. He twitched.

"Fine," he hissed. "I did it. I asked the malpeds to make these flowers grow. It's not that big of a deal."

"You tried to be the master of the earth. That's not our job. And you lied. You lied to all of us. You lied to me! How could you choose these lies instead of being truthful with all of us? We're your tribe. How could you pick lies over that?"

"I'm tired of the work!" Ebert yelled. "I'm tired of the 'needs' of the tribe."

"What are you talking about?" Stella screamed.

"I wanted the festival. I wanted a break. I wanted to make it happen a different way. That doesn't make it wrong. There's nothing wrong with wanting to have some fun."

"What have you done?" Stella screamed. She grabbed his shoulders and shook him hard. Ebert pulled her hands from him and threw them down.

"I don't need you to look out for me anymore. Leave me alone. There is nothing wrong with what I did!"

"Nothing wrong. Nothing wrong. You're letting the

strange things these malpeds do come before what's normal and natural. This isn't right!" Again, Stella shook the root.

Ebert grabbed the root from his sister's hand and threw it on the ground.

"You're just jealous because you didn't figure this out first," Ebert spit. "There's an easier way to get things done, it doesn't have to be all this hard work, all the time."

"Hard work IS the only way," Stella yelled back.

"Not for me," Ebert replied in a deep, slow voice. His eyes burned with anger.

Sister and brother stood and glared at each other; neither spoke. Slowly, Ebert turned away. Stella's stomach lurched.

"Ebert," she said softly. All fight in her turned to fear and worry. "Come back with me Ebert," Stella pleaded. "Just say sorry, start again."

"I don't want to start again. That's just the thing. I don't want to go back to the Trebors. I'm not like you. I don't want to fly with the bird each morning and work all day," Ebert replied. He turned his back to his sister.

"No. Don't say that. That's not all there is. Don't you remember what happens when you're not with the tree? Don't you remember how great it was to get home after the storm?"

"That was all about you, Stella ... never me," Ebert snarled.

"NO! It was about all of us ... it was always about us all!" Stella took a step toward Ebert to grab his arm.

Ebert turned his head and looked at her one more time, his expression stony. His face made Stella shiver. He then spun around and ran.

"Ebert!" Stella screamed. Ebert slipped out of sight into the forest.

Stella stepped forward to go after him, but Snu quickly jumped in front of her.

"Leave him. He has to want to come home himself, he has to apologize because he knows it's the right thing to do, not because you say so. He has to want the tribe for himself," Snu said.

Stella shoved Snu to the side, but there was no sign of Ebert, the forest was silent, he was gone. Stella turned to Snu and collapsed into his arms.

"We have to tell the others," she muttered.

# CHAPTER 13

Stella knew better than to try and find her brother alone. She had learned the hard way what it was like to leave the tree and not rely on the power and strength of the Trebors as a whole tribe. She knew the only way to help Ebert was to talk to Yama and Yapa. Snu had offered to tell them with her, but she wanted to do it alone, and so he had reluctantly left her. And so now, alone, the walk along the curved stairs to her home felt like a great feat, each step took tremendous strength, like rocks were tied to the bottom of her feet, making it hard to even lift them. Her mind spun and she felt sick.

She stood outside the entrance to her home. Her mouth was dry and her eyes stung. She pushed her fist against her eyes to try to get the burning to leave, but it did little to change the feeling. She swallowed and was about to step inside when she heard Yama's voice, "A spectacular day! I'm so proud of our Trebors. I can't wait for Stella and Ebert to be home so we can talk together about the day's festivities. How lucky we are to be here in this mighty tree together."

Stella's legs gave way and she crashed to the floor. She could hear Yama's muffled voice and then felt Yapa's arms pick her up.

"Can you hear me, Stella? Look at me. Can you hear my voice?" Yapa said.

*Yes*, Stella thought. *I hear you*. Her mouth said nothing.

"Put her here," Yama said.

Soft blankets covered Stella. A cool leaf pressed against her forehead. She closed her eyes and fell asleep.

# CHAPTER 14

The smell of kasha bread filled the air, Stella's mouth watered and she smiled as she thought of the delicious taste. She opened her eyes; then she remembered. The taste in her mouth turned sour and she squeezed her eyes shut again.

"Good morning my child," Yapa whispered.

Stella opened her eyes again and looked into her father's face, his eyes were filled with concern. The white streak of fur on his chest caught her attention as the end of it stuck over the top of his shirt. She reached out and touched it. She let her hand rest again Yapa's heart. Yama sat next to her and held her other hand. Stella closed her eyes again and tried to keep the tears from flowing. It didn't work. She couldn't stop her sadness and she couldn't speak.

"It's okay," Yama whispered. Yapa placed his hand over her hand. They sat like this for a while. Stella silently wept. Eventually, Yapa spoke up.

"What happened? Can you tell us?"

Stella sniffed and slowly exhaled.

"Ebert didn't come home last night. Does this have to do with him? Is that why you are so distraught?" Yama said.

Stella slowly sat up. She knew she needed to tell them

everything, but it was hard and frustrating.

"Stella, you know whatever it is, we can work through it together," Yama said. Yapa nodded his head in agreement, but now tears formed at the corners of his eyes as well.

Stella hung her head low and carefully told them about the days that led to this one. She did not leave out a single detail, but spent great attention on each moment of her time with Ebert, each word they said, and how they acted. She spoke of the malpeds, despite her shaky voice, and described the root of the evershi flower as carefully as she could. She told them how she had begged Ebert to return and how he had refused. She felt both relieved and drained when she was finished. Glad to know this worry was no longer just her own, but anxious for something to be done. She wanted them all to fix the mess.

Yama rose after Stella was done speaking and went to the table. She came back with a piece of kasha bread. It was warm and steam rose from it as she tore off a smaller chunk. She handed the piece to Stella and then tore off another one and handed it to Yapa. Stella took a hearty bite, finally hungry after having told her parents everything. Yapa sat perfectly still with the bread in his hand, he did not take a bite but instead stared down at the floor. His thoughts were miles away. Yama rubbed Stella's arm as she chewed. There was nothing to be said yet.

Loud footsteps broke their sad silence. Then Snu stood in the doorway.

"There's a fire near the mubble hole," he yelled. "Hurry!"

Stella, Yama and Yapa jumped to their feet and quickly

followed Snu out of tree and into the clearing. Other Trebors scrambled to join the growing numbers. Yama and Yapa ran straight to Elder Malc who was calling instructions and frantically trying to organize how to put the fire out.

"I need everyone's help!" Elder Malc yelled. "Find every bucket you can and start towards the River Or's east bridge."

"What's happening?" Yama asked.

"One of the bridge's over River Or is in on fire. The one near the Mubble hole," he replied.

"We need more hands," Yapa yelled to the clearing and started organizing groups to move towards the bridge.

Stella only had to glance at Snu to know that he was thinking the same thing she was.

*Ebert! The malpeds! Get to the mubble hole! Fast!*

The two ran as fast as they could. They left behind the frantic voices of the other Trebors who were rapidly making their way to the bridge. They threw themselves through the forest brush and stumbled onto the mossy bed alongside the mubble hole.

Silence.

They both swung their heads around looking for signs of Ebert or the mapleds.

Nothing.

"Where are they?" Stella yelled. "I know they have something to do with this! We haven't had a fire in the forest since the great storm, it has to be because they are back."

"It has to be!" Snu agreed.

But there was no evidence that anything had changed since they left the mubble hole hours earlier.

"We've got to get to the bridge and help," Snu said. "Maybe we'll see something there."

The two made their way to the bridge in no time and pushed through the growing numbers of Trebors helping to quench the fire.

"More water, faster. Make sure it doesn't spread to the forest edges," Yama yelled.

The bridge crackled while red flames licked at the sky above and grew taller and taller by the minute. Soon the flames would catch the leaves of the trees that hung over the bridge and then the forest would quickly follow. Someone threw a bucket at Stella and she jumped into the shallows of the river and plunged it into the water to throw water towards the fire.

Trebors yelled instructions to one another to keep anyone from falling into harm. They fought the fire in unison, each throwing bucket full after bucket full of water onto the burning wood of the bridge. At one point, Stella had to quickly jump back from the flames as she could smell the fur along her forearm singe from being too close.

"Be careful," Yapa screamed to her from the riverbank. He was part of a group that were trying to contain the fire from the top. They were using their buckets to scatter dirt over the fire as well.

All of a sudden, Snu bellowed, "MOVE!"

Stella turned to look behind her and screamed when she saw a huge wave rolling towards them along the river path. They all scrambled towards the river edge. The other Trebors on the river's edge grabbed the hands of those in the river and pulled them out quickly. Stella stumbled on a river rock and slipped under the water. She quickly regained her footing and felt Yama's hand grab under her armpit and pull hard. The water rose around them as the wave got closer.

They threw themselves towards the edge of the river and quickly rolled away as the wave swept past them and engulfed the bridge. It cracked over the bridge and the fire burned out as the huge burst of water swallowed up its fight. The wave broke and crashed back into the river on the other side of the bridge.

Stella watched as the wave petered out and quietly slid away down the river path. She saw a shadow under the surface of the water. She blinked hard to settled her eyes and looked again. There was no shadow. She must have been seeing things. All that remained were tiny sprays of water that flicked along the surface and followed the now small wave as it rode away on the river.

# CHAPTER 15

"Is everyone okay?" Elder Malc asked.

Nods and grunts responded "yes" all around Stella.

"Where did that come from?" Snu asked.

"I've never seen the river do that before," Yapa responded.

Everyone began talking at once. No one had seen the river behave in this way. It was always a slow, rambling river. It never had a force so sudden or tremendous before.

"Did anyone else see a shadow under the water?" Stella asked. "Or anything unusual in the water after the wave left?"

"I only noticed its size," Yama replied.

The others agreed. No one saw anything unusual about the water, other than its size and force. Stella nodded her head and decided she must just be tired and seeing things.

"The good news is that the fire is out," Elder Malc called. "Now we should…"

"Tell them or I will," Snu's voice interrupted Elder Malc.

Snu dragged Rufo to the group as he yelled.

"Now, tell them what you did, tell them what's happening," Snu continued.

Rufo hung his head low and kicked at the dirt at his feet. Tears rolled down his cheek.

"I'm sorry," he squeaked.

"Rufo, do you know what happened here?" Yapa asked.

"NO, but it can't have been Ebert's fault. Or the malpeds. It wasn't Ebert's fault. It can't have been," he mumbled.

"What are you talking about?" Yama asked.

"Is Ebert here? Is he near-by?" Stella added.

"What is this talk of Ebert?" Elder Malc replied.

Yama and Yapa told Elder Malc and the others gathered everything that Stella had shared with them. The group fell silent as they all thought about what these new malpeds might mean, and where Ebert could have gone.

"I'm so sorry," Rufo said again.

"Sorry?" Yapa asked.

"Um, yes, sorry Ebert isn't here," Rufo answered.

"How'd you know that Rufo?" Stella asked. She looked quickly at Snu for an answer, but Snu just stared at Rufo.

"I was watching, I saw everything," he replied.

"You were here with the fire? Or at the mubble hole?" Stella asked.

"Um, at the mubble hole,"

"Tell them everything, or I will," Snu interrupted.

Rufo glared at Snu and his hand began tapping rapidly against his leg and his nose twitched furiously.

"I'm the one who saw the malpeds first," Rufo blurted. "I'm the one who told Ebert. But then Ebert changed and became obsessed with the malpeds. He wanted to go every day to find them. He talked about it constantly. It was his idea to see if the evershi could come early. He asked the malpeds to do it. We didn't know that it would work as it did, or that they would spread like they did. I tried to tell him to talk to you, talk to the Elders, but he refused. I went to tell Elder Malc, but Ebert stopped me. He said he had it all under control. I believed him."

"How could you not tell us?" Stella snapped. "He was in trouble and you said nothing."

"You have to understand," Rufo pleaded. "He was so sure that you wouldn't understand, that you wouldn't let him see the malpeds. He made me promise not to say anything. They aren't bad you see. Well, I didn't think they were bad until I saw how they changed Ebert. He could think of nothing else. When you caught us at the mubble hole he made me think that if we showed you what they could do, you'd like them too, see that they weren't bad. But it didn't work, you still told us to send them away."

"And did you?" Yapa asked.

"I tried. Ebert said no. We fought and I left him. I was in the forest watching what Ebert would do when I saw Stella and Snu come back and confront him. I saw Stella with the evershi root. I knew you understood. But I was scared. So, I hid."

"And the fire?" Elder Malc asked.

"While I was hiding near the mubble hole I fell asleep. I had thought if I waited there long enough Ebert would come back. I woke up to the sound of the fire."

"You didn't see how it started?" Snu asked. He did not seem convinced that Rufo had nothing to do with it.

"I swear, I don't know how the fire started," Rufo

replied. He again dropped his head and shook it.

"Now what?" Stella asked.

"We go home," Elder Malc replied. "There is nothing more to be done tonight. It has been a long day. The news of these new malpeds needs to be discussed. And it sounds like Ebert chose to leave. He was not taken. Is that correct children?"

Stella, Snu and Rufo all nodded their heads yes.

"Then we need to respect his decision," he replied.

"So we don't search for him?" Stella asked.

"No, we wait," Yapa replied.

"Wait?" Snu asked.

"Right now there is nothing we can do but wait. Even if we find Ebert, it does little good if he doesn't want to be here. Ebert has to want to come home. He has to want to live in the tree with all of us. He has to want to leave the malpeds. Until he does, until we have a sign that it is time to intervene, we wait."

# CHAPTER 16

Stella and Fasha sat on the shore of the mubble hole. They both remained silent, comfortable with each other's company and there being no need for words for the moment. The night before had been chaos and Stella was still trying to get her mind wrapped around what was happening. Ebert was gone. The malpeds were gone. The fire at the bridge seemed to have no explanation. And the wave in the river was equally as puzzling and concerning. As hard as she tried to make sense of it all, she just couldn't get any of it to puzzle together in her mind.

*Had Ebert somehow started the fire? Was he with the malpeds? Was the wave in the river just a coincidence of timing?* she pondered.

Eventually, Fasha broke the silence, "Do you think this is a good idea Stel?"

"No," Stella replied. "I'm not sure being here is a good idea. I just don't know what else to do or where to go. This is the last place I saw Ebert and part of me just hopes he'll show up."

Stella closed her eyes and tried to escape the jumble of thoughts that raced around in her head. She realized that today was the first day she hadn't been with the bird in the morning and now she longed for that time. Thoughts of flying with the bird gave her a feeling of peace and she breathed deeply as she stood with her eyes closed. She stayed like this for a while until Fasha grabbed her hand and squeezed it hard.

Stella popped open her eyes and turned to look at her friend. She registered the fear on her face with a jolt of panic. Fasha stared intently at the other side of Stella. Stella swiveled her body to see what she was looking at and came face to face with a line of malpeds. They stood in a tight row next to her with their red eyes bulging and fixed on her; their feet pitter pattered. Suddenly, Stella heaved forward and threw up. She clutched her stomach and heaved again. The malpeds didn't move. Stella drew a breath and tried to calm her nerves. She jumped up and felt instantly light-headed, a roll of nausea took over again, but she still swung her foot at the malpeds. They pitter pattered back ever so slightly and continued to stare at her.

"Go away," she screamed.

The malpeds inched closer and Stella screamed louder. She hollered at the top of her lungs, screaming for someone to hear. Still, the malpeds came closer.

"Fasha, do something," Stella yelled. "Fasha! Fasha?"

As Stella spun around looking for her friend, the malpeds split apart and scurried away. They were everywhere now. Some of them jumped into the water, some ran circles along the shore, others leaped into the air, while others climbed to the treetops and dangled liked bats.

"Fasha!" Stella screamed again. She looked around frantically searching for a hint of where her friend could have gone. There were no footprints and the sound of the malpeds' scurrying around and the pitter pattering of their feet drowned out any other noise.

"Fasha!" she yelled again.

*Nothing*.

A malped flew past Stella's head, another swung from a tree branch and landed in the middle of the mubble hole, a ripple spread in its place, a red ring moved in circles towards the water hole's edge. As the ripples circled to the edge, she heard distinct words in the air around her say, *Play, Play*. She shook her head, it couldn't be, she had to focus, find Fasha.

"Fasha!"

"Here," Fasha's voice finally broke through. "Stel, over here."

Stella looked to where the voice was coming from to see Fasha on the other side of the mubble hole with something small in her hands. She ran to Fasha, her hands over her head, fearing a malped might leap on her.

"What are you doing? We've got to get out of here," she screamed at her friend.

"But look," Fasha said.

There in Fasha's hand was a tiny, tiny malped. It was circled in a tight ball and its little body rose and fell with its breathing; it was asleep. Stella's mouth dropped open.

"It's so sweet, so small, so innocent, look," Fasha said. She held her hand forward for Stella to see the tiny creature.

Stella couldn't focus on the creature, all she could see was that Fasha's fur was not its usual grayish, brown color, but a strange muddy red hue. She knocked Fasha's hand and sent the baby malped flying out, it thumped onto the ground near them.

"What have you done!" Fasha screamed.

"That thing is dangerous, we have to go," Stella yelled back.

Fasha rushed to pick the creature back up and it climbed into the crook of her arm. Fasha crossed her arms in front of her to keep Stella from reaching the tiny creature. The fur on Fasha's chest and arms subtly shifted to the same red color.

Stella steadied her voice and tried to plead with Fasha, "Look at your fur, it's not right, put the malped down."

Fasha turned her back to Stella. Stella could see the red spreading along the fur on her back. All around them more malpeds appeared. They dangled above them from the branches and circled the ground they stood on.

"You have it all wrong, they are good, look at how sweet and small this one is, don't hurt them," Fasha hissed at Stella.

Stella took a step towards Fasha and reached out her hand to her. A rush of wind swept past them and before she could put her hand on her friend, two malpeds wrapped their feet around Fasha's body and pulled her from the forest floor. The hundreds of suction cup feet pulled tightly on Fasha's skin as they lofted her over Stella's head.

"Drop her! Stop!" Stella screamed. She jumped up to try and grab Fasha's foot, but the malpeds flew too quickly.

From high above her, Fasha laughed as the malpeds pulled her up and up. They sat her on a branch far above Stella's head. Fasha's laughter echoed all around. It was a strange sound, one that Stella had never heard from her friend before. The noise was frantic and the pitch was high. Fasha stood on the branch and carefully put the baby malped down, she then reached up to grab onto the outstretched tail of the malped dangling on the branch above her. The malped tossed her into the air and she spun head over heels towards the water in the mubble hole. Just as she was about to splash into the water, another malped jumped out of the water and caught her. They flew into the air. Fasha's laugh became manic and she waved her arms around her head as the malped skidded onto the water and gently placed her on the land on the opposite side of the mubble hole from where Stella was. Fasha stood still. Her laughter stopped and she sat slowly, putting her hands over her face. She dropped her head onto her knees. The malpeds then left as slyly as they came. Quickly they disappeared, leaving Fasha alone, her body a collapsed pile.

Stella's heart raced as she ran around the outskirts of the mubble hole back to Fasha. When she got a few feet from her, she stopped running and walked the rest of the way quietly, approaching slowly. She squatted in front of Fasha and put both her hands on Fasha's knees.

"Are you okay?" she whispered.

Fasha slowly picked up her head and looked at Stella. Her eyes were glassy and tinged with red. Stella stumbled backwards but as she fell Fasha grabbed her hands and yanked her close to her.

"That was amazing," she whispered in a gravelly voice.

Stella was too stunned to speak and too frightened by Fasha's eyes to move. Fasha just stared and smiled at Stella, her hands tightly gripping Stella's. The two sat rooted in their places. Bit by bit, the red in Fasha's eyes receded. They turned lighter and lighter until there was only the faintest hint of pink, and then all the color was gone and they were back to their usual white with Fasha's bright blue eyes sparkling in the center. Fasha let go of Stella's hands. Stella slumped backward and scrambled to her feet.

"I'm so tired," Fasha said, her voice normal-sounding again. She lay her face against the ground and closed her eyes.

"We have to go home," Stella replied. "Get up Fasha."

Fasha carefully sat back-up again and looked shyly at Stella.

"I'm so tired, but that was the most exciting thing I've ever done," she said.

Stella shivered and glanced around her to make sure there were no more malpeds near them. She held out her hand to Fasha and pulled her to her feet. Together they pulled the leaves out of Fasha's hair and brushed the dirt from her fur. Neither spoke. Eventually, they moved away from the mubble hole and headed towards home.

# CHAPTER 17

Four days had passed since Ebert left and the fire had burned at the bridge, and three since Stella and Fasha had been at the mubble hole. Stella knew that Fasha went back every day, hoping to see the malpeds again, and she knew that Fasha took a growing crowd of friends with her each time.

So far, the malpeds had not come back again, but Fasha's story of the tiny malped and all of the fun she had with the other malpeds filled other Trebors' heads with images of amusement and excitement that propelled them all towards the mubble hole. To Stella's surprise, there were even a few adult Trebors who followed Fasha to the mubble hole, in the hopes of experiencing what she did. Stella could not understand how they were able to look beyond the malpeds being the reason Ebert left, and maybe even the fire at the bridge.

There was now an icy silence between the two friends. Stella couldn't fathom why Fasha would continue to tell others such a dangerous tale, always excluding how her fur and eyes changed colors, and only talking about the stunts she did. Her confusion, anger, and worry took over everything, she struggled to do her chores, she couldn't sleep, and even her time with the bird in the mornings had turned into a hunt for Ebert instead of a time of peace. Stella was exhausted and empty.

Regardless, Yama and Yapa felt it was best for Stella to keep working, and with the festival done, the waterspout project seemed the best place for her to spend her time, they decided. Stella was joined by Snu, and the two spent the morning with Elder Malc. Although they did not accomplish much or work up much of an appetite, they sat heavily at lunch, reluctantly eating.

"Love to know what you're thinking," Snu said between bites.

"Waiting is worse than knowing," Stella replied.

"How so?" Snu asked.

"I just wish I knew if he was safe or not."

"Me too. But you know there's nothing we can do now."

"You sound like Yapa and Yama."

"Sorry."

"What if he never comes back?"

Before Snu could answer, they heard a scream from the other side of the tree. Along with the other Trebors in the area, Snu and Stella ran towards the sound. There on the other side of the tree Fasha's mother was on her knees, banging on the ground and screaming.

"No... No... No...!" she yelled.

Snu asked the crowd what happened, and in low voices, they heard how Fasha had left alone that morning for the mubble hole and not returned. It seemed she had disappeared. Other Trebors had gone to look for her, but finding no sign of her, had returned and told Fasha's mother that there was nothing else they could do but wait. A pit grew in Stella's stomach and she found it hard to swallow as she listened to the chatter around her. A hand clasped on her hip, making her jump. It was Yama. Stella could feel tension through her mother's touch.

"Fasha's gone, Yama," Stella said.

"I heard—I must go to her."

Yama pushed through the crowd and sank to her knees with Fasha's mother. She whispered in her ear and then helped her to her feet. The crowd parted as Yama led Fasha's mother through the clearing and into the tree. Stella knew her mother would take care of Fasha's mother in a way that only another mother could. She was the only one that understood the loss and fear that Fasha's mother was feeling, as she too was lost in worry over Ebert.

As the crowd dispersed, Trebors muttered about the malpeds, and much speculation was made about whether Fasha and Ebert were in danger or the lucky ones. Stella felt cold and shivered with anger. She knew the elders would gather right away to talk about what to do and she had to hear what they were saying.

"We've got to be part of the elder meeting," she said to Snu.

"That's not our place," he replied.

"It is this time," she insisted. "We've earned a right to hear the conversation. After everything we've been through … and it's my brother and best friend."

Snu nodded reluctantly and the two walked toward where they had last seen Elder Malc. Not surprisingly, the other elders were already gathering with Elder Malc. Unnoticed, the two stopped nearby and slid into the forest at the back of the gathering. They stooped down and listened.

"Something has to be done to stop these malpeds, they have taken another of our children."

"I don't think they took them, that's the thing, the children chose to go, chose to leave us."

"But it's not safe, others might do the same."

"How can we stop Trebors from going to the mubble hole?"

"The harm of these malpeds is unlike the last time we encountered them."

"They may not even be the same."

"But what if they are? What if they are a new split from the giant malped?"

"No, the giant malped was defeated for good. These malpeds might be similar in form, they might be like the small malpeds we encountered before, but I believe that they are not from the giant malped, that terror was defeated once and for all," Elder Malc said.

There were grunts of agreement.

"Even if their threat is not the same as the giant malped, they are causing harm to our tribe, we can't sit back and watch others be led away like this."

"I agree." Finally, Stella recognized a voice, it was Yapa. "We know what happens when Trebors leave us and the tree for too long."

More grunts.

"We need to find them and remove them," Elder Malc replied.

"How can we remove them? It sounds like they are everywhere and too many to count. We need to make sure others know the danger of leaving the tree, the dangers of the malpeds, but thinking we can get rid of them, I think, is foolish," Yama's voice was loud and clear. Stella pushed her body forward further to see her mother. Yama was walking past them towards the gathering, she was speaking as she walked. "We need to help our fellow Trebors make the right choices, but we can't control all of the forest." Yama turned her head and looked directly at Stella. They caught eyes. Yama turned back to the group, leaving Stella and Snu in their hiding place.

"Elder Malc, I think we should blow the horn, bring the Trebors together, tell them of the danger; but a battle in the forest is not for us," Yama finished.

The elders spoke for a few more minutes, and soon all agreed that this was the best action to take. Yapa quickly moved to call for the horn blast. While Yapa did that, the other elders walked with one another to the clearing to wait for everyone to gather. Yama hung at the back of the group and eventually fell away. She stepped into the brush where Stella and Snu hid.

"I'm sorry," Stella whispered, as Yama stared down at them in their hiding places.

"Don't hide. Be seen. You should be part of this too. You as well, Snu. Come."

Snu and Stella followed Yama out of their hiding place and joined the other Trebors in the clearing. Elder Malc stood on the stump, the bed of moss and flowers that had covered the stump were gone and the entire clearing was back to its usual state, all signs of the festivities were gone, except for a few evershi flowers that littered the ground. The sight of the flower remnants made Stella draw a deep breath to keep from crying. She wondered if she would ever feel as happy again as she had when she was dancing with the evershi chains less than a week ago

"My fellow Trebors, I come to you with words of warning. Warning to stay close to the tree, and not to travel in hunt of the malpeds. I know that the stories of what they can do, and how they can make you feel are tempting, but please trust us when we tell you that nothing good will come of time with those malpeds. We know, from our experience, that the further you are away from the great tree, the more danger you are in, and the less able we all are to help. You must choose to stay here with us, together."

"How do we know they are bad?" a voice from the crowd yelled.

"We don't know their intentions, but we know they tempt you away from the tree and us, and that is never good," Elder Malc replied.

"But how do we know there isn't an easier way, less work, more fun?" another from the crowd yelled. A low murmur spread through the gathered Trebors.

"This is what I worried about," Yama said under her breath.

"You are free to make your own choices, but before you do, I ask that you'll remember the safety and strength of the tree, I ask that you think of the great storm and how it saved us," Elder Malc said with a louder voice.

"To the tree," a voice yelled.

"To the tree!" others echoed.

"Better," Yama whispered.

"To the tree!" a larger crowd rang out.

Elder Malc put up his hand. The crowd quieted.

"Be safe. Work together. Stay close to the tree and one another. And keep hope … hold on to hope for Ebert and Fasha," he said.

Snu put his arm around Stella and she wiped the tears from her face. Her fingers were curled into a tight ball and she slowly released them. Yama pulled her into a tight hug and whispered in her ear, "Be strong with me, don't let yourself fall empty."

Stella nodded and Yama strode away and joined Yapa. They embraced and then joined the other elders again.

# CHAPTER 18

Stella sat at the edge of the clearing and watched as the other Trebors rushed around doing their chores. Snu had gone back to work on the waterspouts, but Stella had chosen to stay at the clearing. She had a feeling, or maybe it was just hope, that something was coming, that maybe Fasha had found Ebert and was bringing him home.

She still couldn't get her head wrapped around them both being lost to the malpeds. Everything around her felt like slow motion and she wondered why everyone felt so far away, even though they were so close. She was near the tree, home with her tribe, yet her mind made her feel like she was miles away. Alone. She would give anything to have her aches go away. The dull pain that sat on top of her head all day, and the tingling that now took over all of her left arm, were starting to weigh on her and she ran through different things she might do to get rid of them.

As she sat still trying to decide what to do next, she felt a cool sensation flow from her waist up through her stomach and along her spine, it slid along her shoulders and down the back of both of her arms. The tingling in her fingers stopped and then the numbness gave way. She turned her head from side to side, delighted that the pain on top of her head also seemed to have stopped. She felt a little like the numbness had been replaced by a burning feeling, but the relief it gave her head seemed worth it. She stretched her arms above her head and then let her hands drop to her lap.

That's when she noticed it. There. On her lap sat a tiny, tiny malped.

It was exactly like the baby malped Fasha had held at the mubble hole. Stella looked around to see if anyone else noticed, but they were all far too busy with their work. Stella was invisible to them at this point.

The tiny malped turned its spiked head towards Stella, rubbed its face against her thigh and purred. Carefully, she placed her hand on its back and felt a quick shock that made the tips of her fingers flicker with red. She smiled and moved her hand all along its tiny body. Its little legs pitter pattered quicker as she petted the tiny creature. She wondered how the baby had made its way to the tree and checked the forest near her to see if any other malpeds lurked nearby. Nothing. *Poor thing must be lost*, she thought.

Just as she had this thought the little malped made a strange sound. She picked it up in both her hands and held it close to her face. It looked like it was sad and made a noise not unlike a cry. She decided she had to take it back to the mubble hole to see if she could return it to the other malpeds. Slowly, she rose to her feet, the malped began to purr again. This made Stella smile. She liked making this tiny creature happy. Its *purrrrrr* made her feel useful. Turning slowly, she took a few steps into the forest. She was now out of sight from the clearing, no one would notice that she was leaving the cover of the tree. Her steps were careful and deliberate; the baby curled in a tight ball in her hands. She now understood why Fasha had been so upset when Stella knocked the baby malped from her hands when they were at the mubble hole. It was so innocent, there was nothing evil about it at all, it just wanted to be held.

Suddenly, out of nowhere, Snu flew into her vision. He jumped towards her, knocking the tiny malped from Stella's hands. She tumbled to the ground. Snu grabbed both of her arms and held her down.

"Get off me Snu. What are you doing?" she screamed.

"Saving you!" Snu yelled back.

Stella struggled under the weight of his arms, but could not get herself free. She looked around wildly to see where the baby malped went, but it was gone.

"Where did it go? Stella wailed.

"Look at me Stel, look at me," Snu said.

Stella turned her head reluctantly to look at Snu. A jolt of fear surged through her veins.

"Oh Snu," she whispered. "I was leaving."

Snu sat back and rocked slightly.

"I saw you walking away from the clearing and when I realized what was in your hands, I knew I had to stop you."

"I don't know what happened," Stella replied. "I just wanted to help it. That tiny creature didn't have a single evil thing about it."

"Except it made you want to walk away from the tree," Snu said.

Stella hung her head low. She hadn't even realized she was walking away from the tree. Somehow, that tiny creature had made her feel that getting it to the other malpeds was most important. She knew now, no one was safe. They could tempt anyone away. Even just a few minutes at the outskirts of the Trebor's home, she had almost been lost like Ebert and Fasha.

"I need to get inside the tree, Snu. I have to rest. I just can't make sense of anything anymore. It could happen to any of us. Any of us."

# CHAPTER 19

"Stella, wake up."

Something hot tickled Stella's nose and she scratched her face with her claws and rolled over. The tickling feeling moved to her ear, so close, so hot.

"Come on … get up…"

Stella pulled her blanket up over her ear.

Cold hands. Her body shook.

"Shhh…"

Stella sat up suddenly and squinted, her eyes adjusted slowly. *Fasha*.

Stella gasped and Fasha pressed her hand to Stella's mouth.

"Shhh…" she said again.

Stella pulled Fasha's hand from her face and widened her eyes to let Fasha know she was shocked and confused.

"I'm scared," Fasha whispered.

"Where've you been? Are you okay?" Stella whispered back.

"I'm okay. I left."

"I know, we've been worried about you."

"No, I mean, I left the malpeds. First, I left the Trebors, and then I came to my senses, and I left the malpeds. I want to be home," Fasha whispered.

Stella threw her arms around Fasha and hugged her tightly.

"You're home now Fasha, you don't have to be scared here."

"But what'll the other Trebors say? I've made a mess."

"They'll just be glad you came home," Stella's voice cracked. "Oh Fasha, I'm so glad you came back." She squeezed her friend harder.

"Fasha?"

The girls jumped.

"Is that you?" Yapa asked into the darkness.

"She's back Yapa, she came back," Stella blurted.

"Was he still there?" Yapa replied, his voice stern.

"Yes, Fasha, did you see Ebert?" Stella repeated.

"He's still there, he's in so deep, he'll do anything to get them to do their stunts," Fasha replied. "I tried to get him to come with me, but he wouldn't, he just stared at me with his shining, red eyes."

"Fasha?" It was Yama now. She embraced Fasha and brushed the hair from her face. "Are you okay? Have you been to your mother?"

"I came here first; I was scared of what they'll do."

Yama joined the girls on Stella's mat and took Fasha's hands in hers, "It took courage to come back. You are brave and strong, there is nothing to be afraid of," she said.

Fasha began to cry quietly and her body sagged.

"Thank you," she squeaked. "I, I, also wanted to give you this," she stammered.

She handed Yapa a pouch. Yama put her hand to her mouth as Yapa slowly reached out for the pouch. Stella gasped.

The pouch had been Yapa's dearest possession for years. During the great storm, Ebert had saved this pouch, not knowing that it contained tiny, powerful seeds from the tree. The seeds in the pouch had been the miracle that gave them the power to defeat the giant malped. For all the years since that day, Ebert had worn the pouch around his neck. It always remained empty, the seeds were not replaced, but to Ebert, and the rest of the family, it was a reminder of what they had been through and the power the tree gave to save them, even in the smallest form of the seeds.

"This is our sign, it's time to intervene," Yapa whispered.

Stella's heart raced and a cold chill ran through her bones. "How do you know?" she asked.

"I think this is Ebert's call for help. The empty pouch isn't enough to save him, he must know this. He needs what belongs inside to battle his way away from the malpeds. He needs us and he needs strength from the tree," Yapa replied.

Stella took the pouch from Yapa and rubbed the brown leather against her fingers. It was worn and soft. A tear slid down her face and fell onto the pouch, leaving a dark stain on its smooth surface. "Do you think we can get there in time now Yapa?" she asked.

"All we can do is try, all we can do is hope that he really does want to come home and believe in the power of the tree," Yama responded.

"Do you think this is really his cry for help? Do you think he really wants to come home?" Stella asked again.

"Like Yapa, I think this is the sign that he is ready for our help, I hope we are right," Yama replied.

Yama stood and motioned Fasha to do the same. Stella quickly climbed to her feet too and reached up to smooth her hair. Fasha hugged Stella, Yama, and Yapa and left to find her family. Left with just her parents, Stella felt she could finally put words to her fears.

"I'm scared we're wrong. I'm scared he doesn't want to leave the malpeds," Stella said. "I was so wrong about him, I thought I could stop him, but I couldn't do anything."

"It has never been your job to make Ebert's decisions for him," Yapa whispered soothingly.

"How can you say that? He's my brother!"

"He's your brother—yes—but he's his own person. You have to let go of thinking you can make him who you want," Yama replied.

"But it used to work, he always looked up to me and listened to what I said."

"Perhaps it was too much, perhaps we all should've let him think more for himself." Yama sighed.

A pain settled between Stella's eyes and she squeezed the bridge of her nose. She stepped back from her parents and put both hands on her knees, then she folded over and put her head between her knees. She drew big gasps of air, over and over until the pounding between her eyes slipped away. Yama had tears in her eyes and her arms fell slack at her side. Yapa rubbed the hair on the top of his head and scratched behind his ear. They looked as awful as she felt.

"All I ever wanted was to love him and protect him," Stella said, her voice now strong and steady.

"That's all we all ever wanted, but sometimes even the

best intentions don't work out," Yapa replied.

Stella nodded and folded her arms across her chest, she rubbed the fur on her arms. "So, we just try, is that it? Hope that the pouch was a call for help?" she asked.

"Yes. Now, now is when we intervene," Yapa said.

# CHAPTER 20

Plans formed quickly. Yapa and Yama called the elders together to discuss how to find and help Ebert. Together, the elders had seen the Trebors through many hard times, and Yama and Yapa knew that the collective thinking would give them the greatest chance to form a plan that would work. They all decided that the best approach was to bring only those closest to Ebert, those whose voice he would hear and respond to most readily.

They considered taking Fasha and Rufo, but in the end, decided against it. Even though they both had the most experience with these malpeds, the elders felt that having them there might confuse Ebert; that it was best to only take those that Ebert hadn't been with while he was with the malpeds. This meant that Snu was the only other Trebor that would travel with Stella, Yama, and Yapa. While Yama and Yapa worked with the elders to prepare, Stella's job was to find out as much as she could from Fasha about where Ebert and the malpeds might be, and how they might approach them.

Fasha had found a tiny malped at the mubble hole and followed it deep into the forest. She had wanted so badly to do tricks with them again that she lost track of where she was going, and just blindly followed the pitter patter of the malped's feet. They traveled deep into the parts of the Or Forest where she could no longer see the great tree stretching into the sky. The canopy of the forest trees and dark coverage of the thick brush made any views to the sky above completely obscured. Fasha said it was dark in the place where she finally saw the rest of the malpeds and Ebert. She couldn't quite place where she had been, as she got lost many times on her way back home. But she was able to point in the general direction she had come from.

When Stella pushed Fasha for more details, she could see that the experience left Fasha drained and confused. She told Stella that when she arrived in the place where the other malpeds were gathered, everything was a whirl of action, just like they had seen at the mubble hole. Malpeds were everywhere. Ebert sat on the forest floor, glazed over, gaping at the action around him. Fasha had instantly been drawn-up into the flurry of fun.

She said the stunts she did were breathtaking, and she and Ebert laughed more than she had in her whole life. Yet, it was the nights, she said, that drove her home. At night, the malpeds slowly disappeared. She couldn't tell where they went, but no matter how much she and Ebert called for them, they didn't return. Without them, they were left cold and hungry. She said that Ebert wouldn't even stay near her, but chose to curl up away from her during the dark parts of the night. He glowed red, she recalled, and twitched furiously all night long. In the mornings, when the malpeds came back, she would forget the painful night and once again enjoy the time with the malpeds.

In the end though, it was late in one of those dark nights, that she suddenly knew she had to get home. She left the malpeds and wandered for hours through the dark forest. Eventually, the moon came out and the canopy of the forest above opened up and she was able to see the sky. It was this opening that enabled her to see the great tree in the distance. From there, with the tree as her guide, she was able to get home. It was not a lot for Stella and the others to go on, but it was enough information to get them started on their journey.

Now, the forest shone as the four Trebors headed across the clearing toward the forest's tree-lined border. It was time to find Ebert. Light reflected from the damp greens that grew alongside the forest path, making their route ahead look magical. The air was still crisp and the sound of the birds, busy in motion above them, took over the space. Behind them, the tree stood tall and strong with its leaves glowing green and its bark shining. The rest of the Trebors gathered at the foot of the tree.

In silence, they each raised a single hand, palms facing forward. Snu stopped before moving into the forest and put his hand up in reply. Stella saw the motion and did the same. Yama and Yapa stopped to look at them, and then walked back into the clearing and raised their hands in response too. Finally, Stella dropped her hand and walked back into the forest, the slow steps of the others followed.

They quickly passed the mubble hole and moved towards the River Or. The bridge had been repaired over the last several days, so crossing the river would not be a challenge. As they approached the bridge, Yapa stopped and reached into his pocket, he pulled out his guiding stone. The color was green and he smiled as he looked at it. Green was a good sign, a sign that they were still connected to the tree and on the right path. He held it up for the others to see. Suddenly, Yama gasped, a red dot formed in the middle of the stone and spread quickly, consuming its entire surface. Yapa dropped it. The stone rolled along the ground and stopped at Snu's feet. It melted halfway into the dirt.

"I've never seen red," Yama gasped.

"We have, once, when we were near to the giant malped's den," Snu replied.

Stella knelt and dug out the stone. She brushed off the dirt against the fur on her thigh and handed it back to Yapa.

"We saw the red right before everything got really bad," she said.

"It's a danger warning for sure," Snu added.

Stella gave a weak smile, there was nothing more to add, they all knew the danger and risk in their journey, the guiding stone just made it more real. Yapa took the stone from Stella's hand and gently put it back in his pocket. A bead of sweat dripped down his cheek and he brushed it away. It left a wet smudge on his fur. Stella pulled out her water and handed it to her father. He took a deep drink, handed it back to her, and nodded. Yama put both hands on the back of Stella's shoulder and squeezed before gently nudging her ahead over the bridge. It was hard to take steps forward with the haunting red of the guiding stone lurking over them.

The smell of fresh wood from fixing the bridge wafted up to Stella's nose as she made her way over the bridge.

Stella had always loved the smell as it reminded her of the many ways the Trebors invented new things for the tribe to use. It didn't surprise her that the bridge was already in perfect condition. Trebors work together well and so jobs were usually completed smoothly and quickly. Even though the bridges over the River Or were not used often, they still needed to remain intact for when they did need to venture into the Or Forest. The bridge felt steadier than ever as they walked across it.

Out of nowhere, a huge wave like the one they had seen days before came barreling towards them. They turned to run off the bridge but the wave was coming to quickly to make it to land.

"HOLD ON!" Yapa yelled.

The four quickly fell to their stomachs and grabbed the edge of the wooden boards on the bridge. Stella dug her claws into them, securing herself as much as she could. She picked up her head to see how long before the wave would hit them and that's when she saw it. The shadow. Looming right behind the wave a dark, diamond shaped shadow emerged. She couldn't see anything else as the water started to pound them. They all gasped for breath and hung on with all their might.

Water churned around them whipping their bodies around. But they held on against the force. Stella legs crashed into Snu's as their bodies flayed around. Then into Yapa's body who was on her other side hanging on. Just when she thought they could not hold on any longer, the rushing water became a smooth wall of icy water. It was arched like the peak of a wave but dark underneath as it swept over them. Then something slick, cool, and slimy flowed over the top of them, followed by what felt like sea weed dragging across their backs as it made its way over the bridge.

In the water around her Stella heard, "Turn back … turn back…"

Then the wave seemed to break and water rained down on them hard, pushing their bodies roughly against the bridge. It was over and they struggled for breath as the waters receded.

"Did you hear it?" Stella huffed, spitting out the water from her mouth.

"Yes," Yama replied

Snu nodded yes as well.

"Turn back," Yapa said. "I heard the words turn back."

# CHAPTER 21

They sat on the other side of the bridge. Wet. Stunned. *Confused.* None of them could make sense of where the wave came from or how they all heard the same words. They stared back across the bridge and wondered if they should turn back like the message had told them. But no, Ebert had reached out for help. He had sent a sign to them. They had to keep going for him. Slowly, they stood and carefully made their way forward.

As they moved through the forest, an eerie silence fell around them. The birds no longer made their busy noises and the forest floor did not echo the scurrying feet of the other creatures. Even the sound of their footfalls seemed to be swallowed by the air around them. The air was thick to breathe and each step felt like a difficult feat. Snu pulled at his ear and Yapa repeatedly rubbed his. Yama kept her head down, deliberately taking step after step. Her movement was slow and steady and Stella tried to follow her lead. It wasn't until Stella picked up her head to look at Yapa and Snu behind her that she realized they were not with them.

"Yapa? Snu?" Stella hollered, but her voice didn't carry.

Yama stopped abruptly and as if coming out of a trance, slowly looked around to get her bearings.

"Did they stop?" Yama asked.

"I don't know," Stella replied. "We need to go back."

The two hurried back along the path they had beaten through the forest and quickly came across Yapa and Snu. They stood like statues in the path in front of them. Dripping down Yapa's face was a thin, sticky looking film that tangled his fur, clumped on his shoulders, and draped under his arms and down the rest of his body. Snu did not have slime dripping down his body but stood up to his knees in a pool of it. They both tried to move, but the slime stuck them to their places and made their movements slow and tiny.

Yama got to Yapa first and tried to pull the sticky stuff from his body, but in the process of it, she too became stuck, her feet glued to the ground by the oozy slime. From above, the slime dripped in front of her and she shifted her shoulder to keep it from landing on the rest of her body. Stella stopped short seeing that the slime crawled along the forest floor in a smooth and neat track. The track that Yapa, Yama, and Snu all now stood stuck in. She carefully avoided falling into the same trap.

"Don't come any closer," Yama yelled to Stella. "If we have any chance of getting out of this mess, we need to make sure you don't get stuck too."

"Where is it coming from?" Snu asked. He could move his upper body, but his wide feet were glued in place. He tried to lift his knee, but it only made the slightest, slowest movement.

Glistening on the forest floor, the track of slime ran from a distance into the place where they all stood, a big pool of slime gathered on the ground around them. But the track stopped there. Carefully, Stella backed up and looked around her, desperate to figure out where the slime was coming from and to find a way to free the others. Her eyes rested on a tall tree that stood over them. There, clinging to the side of the tree sat a bright, orange slug.

The slug was the size of Stella, with smooth skin running along its long body and disappearing into its belly where the slime spread from. Two antennas stood to attention on the top of its head with round, ball-shaped eyes peering from underneath them. It slowly turned its head back and forth. More slime dripped onto Yapa's shoulder and slid slowly down his body. Stella pointed to the slug and the other three shifted their gazes slightly to look at the creature hanging above. It turned its head and lowered its antennas towards Stella. They moved in circles and bowed in the direction where she stood.

"I felt I should stop you," she said.

Stella froze, the slug's voice took her by surprise.

At an excruciating pace, the slug made her way down the tree and along the ground until it stopped in front of Stella.

"I am Swee," the slug said.

"Oh, I'm, ah, Stella," Stella bumbled back.

The slug lay silently in front of Stella while her antennas continued to rotate rapidly. Stella felt anxious to move the slug along so she could find a way to free the others.

"It's, um, nice to meet you," she tried. "It seems we accidentally got stuck in your, um, in your, path," she chose her words carefully.

"It is not an accident," Swee replied.

Stella took a step back and her heart thumped quickly in her chest.

"Stella, move away," Yama yelled.

"No, no," Swee interjected. "Do not run. I am here with a warning. I am not here to harm."

Stella glanced at the others to see if she should believe this creature. They seemed as confused as her. Stella took another step backward.

"I have been watching you make your way through the forest. I know you are looking for the malpeds. I needed to slow you down so you could listen. So I could tell you the truth."

"What truth?" Stella asked.

"The malpeds—they are evil," Swee replied.

"They run through our forest and bring more darkness. They feed off our forest but give nothing back. They want nothing but to survive themselves and do not care who or what they destroy in their path."

"My brother, he is with them, we are trying to find him. Can you help us?" Stella asked.

"I do not want to help you get closer. I want you to go back," Swee whispered.

Stella dropped slowly to her knees to be level with Swee's eyes. She peered into them. They were a soft yellow color with a rim of orange, they held nothing but kindness in them.

"You slowed us in your slime to warn us to turn back?" she asked.

The slug nodded her antenna eyes, *yes*.

"Thank you Swee, but we can't turn back, not without my brother."

"These creatures, they are destroying our forest, our homes are wasting away, they will do the same to you," Swee urged.

"Please, help us. Don't stop us," Stella responded.

Swee rotated her body towards Yama, Yapa and Snu, her slimly body a u shape as she focused her attention on them. Then she slid her way back to facing Stella.

"You brought leaves from your great tree I assume?" Swee asked.

Stella reached into her pack and pulled out a leaf.

"Place it at the end of my trail," Swee directed.

Stella walked to the back of the slug where the trail disappeared underneath it. She carefully placed the leaf on top of the slime. A green ripple spread from the leaf into the slime. Like a surging river, the green flowed into the slime and ran along its path. The green spread into every inch of the slime, including the slime that dripped off Yapa. A pungent smell lifted from the slime and circled in the air around them. Bit by bit, the slime turned to small, green granules. Snu and Yama lifted their feet and shook the granules from their claws and fur. Yama shivered his body and sent green pellets flying from his fur. They all ran to stand next to Stella and Swee.

"You really are good, aren't you?" Snu asked.

Swee bowed her head. "I don't want you to perish. Be warned. Be careful. There is great danger."

Stella slid her hand into Yama's hand, Yapa placed his hand on Snu's shoulder.

"You risk all for the one?" Swee questioned.

"Yes. We do," Yapa replied.

Swee picked up her head, her antennas searching the air around it.

"Then I have said all I can. May your journey not end in despair."

With this, Swee turned her body and slowly slid away. The four stood in silence watching as this mysterious slug carefully made her way back into the forest brush. Her progress was slow, but they did not make a move until she was well into the woods. Instead, they remained still and took in the warning of this kind slug, as well as the creepy silence that gathered around them.

# CHAPTER 22

Yama turned and headed back in the direction they had been walking as if nothing had happened. They all followed, walking on in silence again. They had now been strangely warned twice to turn back, but they all knew, without speaking, that they wouldn't. They had been willing to wait for Ebert to make his own choices, but now that he seemed to reach out for help, they would do whatever it took to help him home.

Soon, Snu began to rub his ears again and Yapa shook his head repeatedly. Stella heard a buzz in her ears and rubbed them as well. No change. She rubbed again. Nothing. The buzz took the place of any forest noise. In fact, it was if there was no noise at all. Just the buzzing in her ears.

"I can't hear the forest life," she finally said.

"Neither can I. It's like all of the animals and creatures just stopped. Nothing is moving or making any sound," Snu replied.

"As it is with me," Yapa added.

They kept walking, but the only noise to fill their progress was the sound of their feet along the path and the buzzing in their ears. The cracking of the branches and crinkling of the leaves underfoot seemed muffled by the heavy atmosphere. Even the smell in the air shifted. The fragrance of the evershi flowers no longer greeted them. Instead, they were enveloped by a rancid, still air. The silence and the piercing smell drove deep into Stella's mind and she wondered if they had been right to go looking for Ebert after all.

Yama pulled the front of her shirt over her nose to shield against the smell. Snu coughed loudly trying to clear the thick air from his throat. Yapa pulled a leaf from his pocket and handed it to Snu. Snu put it to his nose and breathed the scent in with a deep inhale. He handed it to Yama and then to Stella who both did the same. The colorful tickling of the tree's fresh scent crawled up Stella's nose and settled in her mind. All at once she felt calmer about pushing forward. She also noticed that the buzzing in her ears settled.

That's when they heard it … the hissing.

It clung to the stale air around them, enveloping them as they walked.

*Hisssssss.*

Snu gasped, his eyes wide.

"It can't be," Stella muttered. "It's not the same."

"Not the same," Snu repeated. "Can't be the same."

This sound. The hissing. It hit them like a thunderbolt. It was the same noise that had taunted them under Mt. Bor. Stella had fought to banish this awful noise from her memory, but the hint of it in the air around her brought her right back to the fear that had gripped her heart when they fought the giant malped all those years before.

"Can't be the same," she said again.

All of a sudden, they heard rustling in the bushes nearby. Sound came rushing back into the space all around them. The noises of the forest were magnified now, the hissing bold and everywhere. They jumped around and crouched with their backs to each other in a circle. They waited. A branch snapped. The leaves in the forest bristled. A streak passed in front of them. Red swirled above. The hissing grew louder. The trees that hung above them shook. Then, silence. The hissing left, the sounds of the forest once again somehow swallowed by the air around them.

EYES. RED EYES. They glowed from the forest brush. But they were bigger than the eyes of the small malpeds. The group backed in closer, now a tight circle. They could feel each other's heavy breathing. The eyes got closer. They did not belong to a malped.

*It was Ebert.*

Yama gasped and Yapa grabbed her wrist to steady her from jumping at Ebert. No one moved. Ebert crawled out of the bushes on all four towards them. His fur was matted and his hair stood wild on top of his head. As he crawled, his legs were straight and sent his hind end high above him, covered in dirt and tangled with leaves. His arms were low to the ground and his claws scraped the earth. He moved toward them, leaving a trail of lines along the earth as he crept. He locked eyes with Stella and kept them trained on her as he paced in front of them, back and forth, staring. He jumped back suddenly.

Yapa yelled, "Son!"

Ebert cocked his head and glared at Yapa. He then began circling them, slowly. He made rings in the dirt with his claws.

They spiraled around them getting closer with each turn. Stella stepped forward, her foot touching one of the rings in the dirt, she was careful not to place another foot out of the rings. She turned her body to face Ebert as he circled back. He stopped.

"It's me Ebert, Stella … it's us … your family … come back to the tree with us," she pleaded.

"Did you bring it?" Ebert asked, his voice was raspy and unfamiliar.

No one replied.

"Did … you … bring … it?" he said again, his eyes burrowing into Stella as he spoke.

"Bring what?" Yapa asked.

Ebert jumped back again, outside of the rings he had carved into the ground. He turned his attention to Yapa.

"My pouch," Ebert said.

"You mean *my* pouch, the empty pouch you have been wearing?" Yapa asked.

"YES!" Ebert yelled in reply. "MY pouch,"

"Come home Ebert," Yama whispered. "We have the pouch, come home, let us help you."

"I WANT MY POUCH!!!!!" Ebert yelled.

Yapa fumbled with his pack and slowly pulled out the pouch. He held it by its long leather cord; the pouch dangled at the bottom. Ebert pounced towards Yapa and snatched it from his hand. He crawled quickly away from them , yanked open the pouch, and tipped it upside down. Nothing came out. He shook it. Nothing. He pulled harder at the opening, turning it over and shaking it again and again.

"IT'S EMPTY!" Ebert hollered.

"Yes, you sent it empty with Fasha, that's why we came for you," Stella said.

Ebert crouched lower and shook violently. "I sent it with Fasha so it would get filled. Seeds, I need the seeds."

"Come with us, if it's seeds you need, there are more than you can ever want back at the tree," Stella pleaded.

"I don't want to go back to the tree. I want seeds now, here!" Ebert yelled.

Yama took a step closer to Ebert and he growled. The growl was low, gravely and dark sounding. Yama reached out her hand and he recoiled further. She took another step and extended her hand.

Again, Ebert growled.

"I need seeds for tricks," Ebert muttered.

"Come with us son, come back," she said.

Ebert backed away slowly, his growl grew deeper and more intense, rolling out from the back of his throat.

"I need acorns for tricks," he said again.

Yama lunged towards him and attempted to grab his arm.

"No," Yapa yelled. "Not like this!"

Yama missed and fell forward, her cheek hit the ground first. Ebert stood upright and looked down at his mother. Yama pushed herself up onto her knees.

"Please, we love you, come home," she begged.

Ebert shook harder, the fur running along his back stood on end. He stared at Yama on her knees in front of him and growled.

Then.

He lunged.

# CHAPTER 23

Snu screamed.

The brush around them bristled and shook.

Ebert had lunged away from them at the last second, sparing his rage from Yama. Relief swept through Stella when she realized that Yama was unharmed and still sat on her knees in front of them. Yapa ran towards the noise and flew into the dense forest. Stella took two huge strides and dropped to her knees to join her mother. Snu flew past her and followed Yapa into the forest. Ebert had disappeared so quickly it was hard to tell which way he went.

"No … no … no…" Yama moaned. Her face was pushed against her palms, pressed into the dirt of the forest floor, her body was folded in two.

"He looked at me like he doesn't even know me," she wailed.

Stella sat next to her mother. Pain pulsed up her left side and ended over her left eye, it was so intense it made it hard for her to form any words to comfort her mother.

"How can this be … how can it be?" Yama moaned again.

Stella put her hand on her mother's back, she didn't move it, just left it still, her fingers spread wide. There were no words to say she realized. All she could do was be with her.

The leaves and branches around them shuddered again and Yama sat up quickly. Stella dropped her hand and looked around, scanning the forest. Snu pushed through the brush and Yapa followed behind. Yama jumped to her feet and looked at them hopefully, but Yapa dropped his head and Snu shook his. Yama sunk again to the ground where Stella had remained sitting.

"He's gone," Yapa said.

"We tried to catch him, but he was too quick," Snu added.

"He didn't want us to catch him, that was never his plan," Yapa said.

"I shouldn't have lunged for him," Yama whispered. "He was just so close, I wanted to hold him, help him."

Yapa and Snu slowly sat with Stella and Yama. Yapa pressed his forehead to Yama's.

"You know that wasn't your fault," he said.

"It was. I should have stood still. I should have waited for him to reach out," Yama replied. "I just couldn't."

"He never had any intension of touching us," Yapa answered.

"He's right," Stella added. "You could see in his eyes that it wasn't really him. He just wanted the seeds, not us." She rubbed the left side of her neck trying to stop the pain from circulating into her head.

"What was it he kept saying?" Snu asked.

"I need them for tricks," Yama croaked.

"Tricks?" Snu said.

"He knew we'd see the empty pouch as a sign that he wanted help. He knew that it would bring us to him. He just assumed we'd bring it full of seeds. He was using us to get his hands on them, I'm sure of it," Yapa said angrily.

"How didn't we see this coming?" Yama asked.

"I don't understand," Stella said. "See what coming?"

"He made it seem like he wanted help from us only to get what he wants from us," Yapa replied.

"I should've known it was too easy," Yama cried. "I just so wanted to believe he was ready for help, and that he was reaching out to be saved from whatever the malpeds have over him."

"But I don't understand why he needs seeds for tricks. What did he mean?" Snu asked again.

"It's them," Stella yelled suddenly.

"It's who?" Snu replied.

"It's them ... it's them," Stella repeated.

"I asked why he needed the seeds, I know it's the malpeds he is with," Snu replied.

"No! It's them! It's the same malpeds ... don't you see it?"

Snu blinked and leaned back from Stella. His mouth dropped open slowly.

"She's right," Yama whispered. "It is them."

Stella shook her head wildly. "How are they alive?"

"You're not saying what I think, are you?" Yapa asked.

"Yapa, these malpeds are the same evil we faced, it's the only explanation," Stella replied. "Their tricks are what made Ebert follow them, but the minute he was fully hooked on being with them, they must've stopped the tricks and told him he needs seeds for more."

"All they ever wanted was the tree's power," Snu added.

"Yes, they must see Ebert as a way to get it," Stella let her words trail away. She closed her left eye and focused on Yapa with her right eye, the pain in her head was unbearable now.

"I thought we had defeated the giant malped and the evil that ran from it once and for all, I truly thought it was over for good," Yapa said.

"I did too," Yama replied. She spoke so quietly that Stella could barely hear her.

"What do we do now? We can't just leave him again," Stella said.

"We have to. If we are right, and I know in my heart we are, the evil of the malpeds is too much for us to conquer alone, the evil once again used trickery to confuse, and this time Ebert fell victim to its allure. I fear the worst for him," Yama replied, her voice cracked as she spoke.

"Don't say that Yama. We have defeated them before, we can do it again. We just need to get back to the other Trebors and make a plan, gather the seeds of the tree as our defense," Stella said.

"It is different this time," Yama said. "We don't know if they take on an evil form as they did before."

"What do you mean? We saw it, the small malpeds form the giant malped," Snu replied.

"Last time, yes. But we don't know what form the evil

is taking this time or if it morphs at all. It seems a new evil has sprouted from the death of the giant malped. The small malpeds look the same as those you followed and then battled after the great storm, but we don't know that they are, or what evil lurks within them," Yama explained.

As they spoke, the pain in Stella's head became too much to bear and she lay down on the earth in front of Snu and her parents. She pushing her head against the ground and it gave her a small amount of relief. Her mind swirled and flashes of the battle she had fought against the giant malped pushed its way to her mind. She saw its bulging red eyes and scaly skin, the glare from its black crown sitting among the spikes of its enormous head. As the memory flashed in her vision, the pain in her head grew worse. The memory of its cold breath and the feel of its fist clutched around her body made her tremble.

*How is it not dead? I saw it collapse ... what kind of worse evil comes from that kind of dark death?* she thought.

"Stel, we've got to go," Snu whispered, his face suddenly close to Stella's on the ground. "We need to get help; we need to warn the others."

"Is he lost forever Snu?" Stella asked, her face still pressed to the ground.

Yama gasped and Stella realized they were all listening. She sat up and looked at her mother's strained face. She had never seen fear in Yama's face like this before. Fear and pain. Stella lifted her eyebrow in the hope of getting a response, some reassurance.

"I don't know," Yama whispered in response. "I don't

know."

A shadow swept over the space surrounding them. They looked up but couldn't see where it came from. As quickly as it covered them it slyly drifted away. They looked at each other in silence and without speaking stood and slowly began retracing their steps back to the tree.

# CHAPTER 24

"Seal the doors!" Elder Malc's voice boomed throughout the hollow of the tree. Trebors lined the circular stairway and peered from their homes. "All Trebors are to stay inside the tree, no one is to leave," he bellowed.

It was warm and bright inside the tree. Families had been tucked into their homes and the smell of evening meals, left uneaten on family tables, wafted into the opening of the tree's hollow.

"We believe the threat of great darkness looms again and the only way to ensure our safety is to stay together here in our home. We still do not know the depth of the threat, so please heed this warning. The elders are gathering and will make a plan," Elder Malc continued.

Stella stood on the bottom floor of the tree next to her parents, Snu, and Elder Malc. The ache in her head had subsided as she got closer to home, and now that she was within the tree the clutching hand of pain had let go and she could once again see clearly. She looked up into the colony of Trebor homes as Elder Malc spoke. The brightness that poured out from the homes, and the open, wide faces of her fellow Trebors, made it hard to believe that any darkness could threaten them. She knew here in the tree they were all safe, but Ebert was not there. He was in the hands of this darkness, away from the only place Stella knew to be truly safe. Also, at some point, the Trebors would need to go outside of the tree to tend to the field crops and waterspouts.

Something had to be done. They couldn't ignore the truth that evil was creeping its way throughout the lands of Bori. Yama shivered next to her and Stella slid her hand into hers. It was cold. The expression on Yama's face was blank. Stella tried to get her mother to respond by squeezing her hand, but Yama remained unmoved.

"And now, with the doors sealed, I wish you all a safe night," Elder Malc concluded.

Quiet murmurs filled the space around them but no one moved. The concerned faces of their fellow Trebors reflected their worries. As one tribe, the Trebors held the pain of loss. Ebert wasn't just lost to Stella and her family; he was lost to them all. They all grieved this sadness, just as they all feared the darkness of it. The threat that laid outside the tree, the evil that lurked in Bori, was one that came for them all, not just Ebert. The faces of the Trebors reminded Stella that only together could they survive this, that only together could there be any hope of bringing Ebert back.

Elder Malc interrupted the silence, "I believe you need rest and food before we speak further." He directed his comment to Yama but she didn't even seem to notice he spoke at all. Stella squeezed her hand again, but she didn't move.

Yapa quickly jumped in to reply for her, "Yes … we need some time… We'll find you shortly … after we process a bit."

Elder Malc nodded and turned to Snu, "Will you help me gather the other elders? We will meet in the Inner Hall." Quickly Snu scurried away to find his mother, father, and the other elders.

Stella, Yama, and Yapa walked up the staircase toward their home. Their fellow Trebors parted to make room for them as they traveled up the winding steps. Their faces registered the pain Stella felt, the pain she knew her parents felt, but they also reflected hope, and this gave Stella's step a less heavy feeling as she wove her way up the stairs. At least they were not alone, and for now, they were safe in the tree.

When they got to the landing outside of their home, Yama and Yapa ducked inside quietly without looking back at the Trebors gathered around them. But Stella stopped to let them know that she was grateful for their support. As she faced the group of Trebors standing on their landing, she noticed that Rufo was among them. He hung back from the crowd, his head hung low, his shoulders slumped, and his ears flat against his head. Slowly, the crowd dispersed until it was just Rufo left standing in front of Stella.

"Rufo," Stella said. It was all she could get out. She threw her arms around him, trying to get some comfort from Ebert's best friend. He clung to her.

"I, I, I'm sorry … I just wanted to say I'm sorry." Rufo stumbled over his words as he fought back his sobs. He spoke over Stella's shoulder as they stood, arms wrapped around each other.

"It's not your fault," Stella replied. She carefully pulled back from Rufo's embrace. She wanted to really mean these words, but still couldn't help but feel some anger at the sight of Rufo. It had been Rufo who encouraged Ebert's time with the malpeds, it all began with the two of them. Although, even as she thought these things, she knew Ebert had made his own choices.

"I just wish I could help, wish I could make it right, bring him back," Rufo continued.

"Me too," Stella muttered in response. The two stood in silence for a moment before Stella patted Rufo's shoulder and ducked inside her home to find Yama and Yapa.

Inside her home, everything looked the same. Their wooden chairs were set neatly around their table. The hearth, although cold, was well swept with new logs sitting, waiting to be used to make yaza cider or flanut tea. Stella's stomach growled. She squinted her eyes to look beyond their common room and into the sleeping space she shared with Ebert. His mat lay on the floor, unused for weeks, her mat lay nearby with blankets askew where she had gotten up quickly with such hope earlier. Yama and Yapa sat heavily in their rocking chairs near the hearth. They did not speak to each other or turn to look at Stella.

"I'll make us something to eat," Stella said. Although neither of her parents replied, she made herself busy. She lit the fire and put tea in the pot to warm. She pulled a brightly colored, purple quinold from the shelf and sliced it carefully. She didn't have the energy to cook it, but it would do to fill their empty stomachs. Yama held the food on her lap, but made no move to eat anything. Yapa sipped his tea. Stella sat at the table and watched her parents. She forced herself to eat and drink, but the yaza lumped in her throat and the tea burned her tongue. Outside their burrow, Trebors spoke in hushed tones, but no one entered their space.

Together, but each so alone, the three sat. Stella wondered what they had done wrong, what they had missed. They had thought that Ebert had called for help, but instead he wanted to use them. She burned with anger that she had never felt for her brother before. Instead of feeling sadness, Stella found her cheeks hot with rage as she watched her parents. They sat like stone, broken and silent, and it was Ebert's fault.

# CHAPTER 25

The night passed and Stella woke to a knock at the entrance of her home. She peeked her head outside to find Elder Malc and Snu standing on the outside landing. They both wore grim expressions. Snu looked as miserable as Stella felt.

"How are your parents, child?" Elder Malc asked.

Stella peered back into her home. Yama and Yapa did not stir, but remained unmoved, slumped asleep in their rocking chairs. They hadn't even had the energy to lay down on their sleeping mats. The creaking of the chairs had echoed in their home all night, as both had tossed and turned fitfully. Now, though, they were so still that they looked completely unreachable in their sleep.

"I can wake them, but I'm not sure they'll be able to hear anything you have to say," Stella replied.

"Are they that bad Stel?" Snu asked.

Stella pounded her fist against her leg and then threw open her hands in front of her.

"They're so broken. He broke them," she said.

Elder Malc's eyes creased and he nodded his head slowly.

"Child, Ebert did not do this to your parents," he said.

"He did! If it weren't for him, they'd be leaders still. Now, they can't move, they are hollow," Stella replied.

"Just like you thought you could save him, they did too. And just like you had to come to the truth that he'll only be saved if he wants to be, they have too as well."

"But they knew that. They told me. That's why we didn't do anything until Fasha returned with the pouch. We thought he was reaching out for help," Stella said.

"Yes, but he wasn't," Snu added.

"I know, but they waited, they knew he had to want to be saved," Stella tried.

"Child, they—"

"I'm not a child Elder Malc," Stella interrupted. "Stop calling me one."

Elder Malc was visibly taken by surprise at Stella's outburst and Stella felt instantly ashamed.

"I'm sorry," she whispered.

"No, you are right, you are not a child," Elder Malc replied. "I was trying to bring comfort, but I see that what you need are clarity and truth."

"Yes," Stella agreed.

"Your parents knew they couldn't save Ebert without him wanting to be helped. The power of the tree can bring him back, but he has to want that. Only his desire to accept help from a deeper source can truly free him from the evil that has taken him over. Even together, we can only help if he wants to be with us. And yet still, your parents were hopeful. They thought they saw a sign because they wanted one so badly. We all did. We all hoped the pouch was it. Sadly, they—well, all of us—are facing the truth that it is never as clear as that." Elder Malc continued, "Stella, you can't save them from that truth, just as much as you can't save Ebert from the grasp of this evil force. You can't fix him."

"Then what can I do?" Stella asked.

"You must start by not letting anger take over your heart. Ebert is not himself. He is not intending to hurt you or your parents," Elder Malc answered.

"And we've got to just move on for now," Snu added. "We can't go after him. The elders talked about it late into the night last night. We can't risk putting more Trebors so close to the malpeds as we don't know the large form that their evil takes this time. And we can't save Ebert if he doesn't want to be saved. So, we must move forward with our daily routines and hope for his return. We'll go back out and tend to the crops and all of our work, but won't leave the tree's cover." Even as Snu tried to speak with certainty, his face showed the sadness he too felt as he delivered this information to Stella.

Stella let the news settle in. Her mind darted to different solutions and back again, but she knew that what Snu said was the only real response. With a resigned sigh, she responded, "I'll tell my parents. It'll be better if they hear the tribe's response from me."

"So be it," Elder Malc replied.

He hugged Stella and turned back to the staircase. With very deliberate steps, Elder Malc made his way from floor to floor down the circular stairs. The weight of the situation hung on him as well and his footsteps were heavy on each rung of the stairs. When he finally reached the bottom, he crossed to the mighty, arched doors and stood still in front of them. Stella and Snu leaned over the landing edge to watch closely. He pointed to the doors and a group of Trebors standing nearby rushed to open them. They pushed on their heavy bark laden slabs and daylight streamed through the opening.

The light grew larger and larger, as the doors allowed its splendor to fill the hollow of the tree. Elder Malc stood in the bright spotlight of the sun, pulled the signal horn from his pack, and blew into it. Everyone stopped what they had been doing and turned their attention to the sound of the horn. Elder Malc lifted his hand above his head, his palm facing where Stella and Snu stood. He gazed up at them as he spoke.

"Today is not easy. But today we move forward again. Stay diligent and aware as you go about your daily routines. Do not travel far from the tree and stay close together," Elder Malc's voice echoed throughout the space around them.

Stella glanced back into her home, but her parents were still not stirring. She knew they heard the horn, no one can miss it, yet, they made no attempt to move. Both Yama and Yapa stayed in their silence, clinging to the safety of their closed eyes.

"What do I do?" Stella asked Snu. She felt exhausted and empty.

"Nothing. You go about your routines. You push on. You hope that Ebert picks up his head and sees the tree. You hope that he remembers its power and the love of his tribe. But until then, there is nothing to do but wait and stay together," Snu replied.

"Yama and Yapa, should I tell them what is happening?"

"They heard. I'm sure they heard. But they might not want to let it in yet," Snu replied. "Maybe they need the space to let this all settle in?"

"I should fly," Stella responded. "I'm going to find the bird. Maybe from there I'll find the courage to do the hardest thing of all."

"The hardest thing? Snu asked.

"Be still," Stella replied. "Do nothing, wait."

Snu nodded. He knew better than anyone how little Stella liked to wait. How hard it was for her not to whirl into action.

"How about if I come with you?" Snu asked.

"No. I need to be alone. Just like I can't save Ebert, you can't fix this for me either."

"I wish I could…" Snu muttered quietly.

Stella hugged Snu and whispered, "Thank you, I know."

She turned and scurrying down the stairs and out into the morning sunshine, leaving Snu standing on the landing watching.

The light was so bright out that it alarmed Stella. She wondered how it could be so bright out when so much darkness lurked all around them. An evershi flower fluttered past her, remnants of the festival long gone, another lifetime ago for Stella. The wind carried the fragrance on its wings. And though the scent usually made Stella smile and feel joyful, now she only felt resentful. She turned her back to the other Trebors gathering in the clearing outside the tree. She didn't have the energy to speak to anyone and felt more resentment that they were not bearing as big a loss as her. She wiggled her hands to try and rid herself of the anger, but it was already creeping along her skin and making all of her feel terrible. The only thing she knew to do was climb, climb to the tree's top and hope for the bird.

So, she made her way carefully up the tree, gazing above her at the sun-drenched clouds that lightly touched the tree's mighty reach. The bark felt warm on her hands as she climbed, and the smell of home filled her lungs. As she climbed higher, she too mingled with the clouds. The clouds seemed to soak up the sun, but also the calm green of the tree. They held the peace of the tree and warmth of the sun as they swirled around Stella. She took in the sight and hoped it would sway her heart from the growing anger and sadness.

She hoped the bird would come for her. And just like that, it appeared. A warm breeze blew through her fur before she even reached the top of the tree. The bird glided past her, circling the tree. She swiveled her body and reached her hand out into the cloudy sky. The bird circled to her and she grasped onto the feathers on its wing and flung her body up onto its back. Instantly, she felt warm and safe. She laid her head on the bird's back and closed her eyes. The bird flew.

# CHAPTER 26

Stella struggled to get rid of her anger towards Ebert and let the peaceful flight settle-in. She yelled and screamed into the bird's feathers. She shook her fists and yelled some more. And slowly, very slowly, her fight swept away, as if on the wind they flew on. She felt tired, but no longer hung on to the rage that was threatening to take over. Now, with more calm, Stella looked out at the land of Bori as she soared through the sky.

The evershi had now spread far beyond the mubble hole and no longer grew alone. With them, sprigs of other flowers popped out their early leaves and climbed up forest trees and along riverbeds. It all looked so different to Stella from the last time she had flown with the bird. She had been so busy worrying about Ebert that she had forgotten that the land of Bori still grew. The power from the tree had saved Bori after the great storm by pushing its warmth into the ground, feeding the land so it could grow back. It had been a spectacular thing to watch and Stella remembered the joy it brought her after the storm to see the land around her come back to life. *And yet,* she thought, *were the malpeds alive that whole time? Had they been lurking while the Trebors all thought they were gone for good?* She pushed her head further into the bird's feathers and felt the dark thoughts drift away again. *It will get better*, she now thought, *somehow it will be okay.*

After some time like this, Stella picked up her head to see where they were. To her surprise, they had blown towards Mt. Bor. They never went this far, the bird usually swept in mighty circles over Or Forest and Vern Valley, but not to the mountain. Stella placed her hand over her eyes to see more clearly, the bird flew so fast that tears formed at the corners of her eyes from the rushing wind.

"Slow, bird, slow," she yelled. The bird did not slow down.

"Why are we going towards Mt. Bor? This is too far from the tree. I don't want to see the old trunk or the ruble of the giant malped. Turn back!" she screamed.

The bird pushed up its wings and plowed them down even harder than before; it gained more speed. Stella dug her hands further into its feathers and lowered her body to brace herself against the wind. Far too quickly, the base of Mt. Bor appeared, then the towering form of the dead trunk came into her vision.

"Why?" she yelled again.

Faster they flew. More tightly she gripped. Her nose stung as an awful smell caught in the air around her. And although she still felt warm atop of the bird's wide back, the air around her was suddenly cold and the clouds now hung low and gray.

Then she saw it.

Red. Streaks of red light spraying into the sky out of the old trunk. She rubbed her eyes, but they were not playing tricks on her. Her mouth dropped open and her heart picked up its speed. The bird slowed. Under them, the stony pile of the collapsed giant malped lay in the field. It was still there as she remembered it. Each stony part of the giant lay as it had when she flew from this place so many years before. No Trebor had ever been back. It was against the tribe code now. As far as she knew, no one had dared to break this code. The scene of the giant malped's demise was etched into Stella's memory, and hovering above it was like living that day all over again. Except this time, she had a different fear. She wasn't afraid of the giant, he still lay there dead, harmless. But there was a red glow that bounced from its form. It matched the glow that reached out of the trunk behind it. It was this sight that made the fur on Stella's arm stand to attention. Somehow, she knew that this, the stony form with its red glare, and the trunk with its warning of color, was the source of the new evil. The evil that took over Ebert.

"We have to go back," she yelled to the bird. She had seen enough. She knew the bird had brought her there to show her where the evil started from, and she had no doubt the malpeds too came from this awful sight. "Now!" she yelled louder.

With great speed, the bird tore through the sky, a quiver rippling through its wings. Stella pushed her entire body as close to the bird as she could. She had never known it to move with such speed, and the urgency made her heart race. She could not open her eyes to even look at the land below her. All she could focus on was the sinking feeling that gathered in her stomach at the same speed that the bird flew. She had to let the others know that these tiny creatures that looked just like the malpeds they met in the past, were different than what they experienced before.

They were not part of the giant, for he still lay dead in the field, but they came from the evil that oozed out of him, of that she was sure. How different this evil felt from the collective form of the giant she had battled. She could only imagine with dread the type of darkness these new malpeds represented, and she knew she couldn't bear this knowledge alone.

Stella forced herself to pick up her head and look to the tree. It grew bigger as they flew closer. But something was hovering over the tree. She had never seen another bird the size of the one she flew on; she had always believed there was only one great bird. Yet over the tree, vast wings spread in the air, the shape of a bird emerged. No colors jumped from its body, but a red glow hung on the tips of its wings. They drew closer and from the sky high above she could see Trebors running, screaming and pointed to the bird above the tree.

"What are they doing?" she yelled to the bird. "Why are they scared? We're too far away, we've got to get to them."

The bird shape in the distance lunged out of the sky suddenly, its beak pointed towards the earth. It spiraled in circles towards the ground, a rocket of speed aimed at the Trebors below.

"Stop!" Stella yelled. Her voice just drifted into the air above her, no one could hear her from such a distance. She watched in horror as the bird propelled itself towards the ground. The scene below was horrifying, Trebors tripped and fell as they tried to run to safety. Children were dragged by their parents, and the elders ran in circles unable to stop the panic. Then suddenly, the bird raised up its head and leveled out. It flew just a few feet above the ground.

On its back sat a Trebor.

There was no mistaking the figure.

*It was Ebert.*

# CHAPTER 27

Ebert shook his hands wildly above his head. His head swung back and forth manically as he watched the Trebors below scatter in all directions. He leaned back on the bird and it flew straight up into the sky again. It hovered above as Ebert watched what was happening on the ground from his perch. He cackled and rocked back and forth as he watched the scene below him. Elder Malc stood in the middle of the clearing and stared straight up at Ebert. The rest of the Trebors continued to run towards the tree's opening. Elder Malc raised his hands into the sky and stood like a statue reaching for Ebert. Yama and Yapa ran from the tree's arched opening towards Elder Malc and threw up their arms into the air as well.

In no time at all, the crowd of frantic Trebors realized what was happening, and drew together next to Elder Malc. They all pushed their open hands in the air towards Ebert. Ebert's crazy motions and cackling stopped for a brief moment. Silence filled the sky. Ebert jerked again, but this time his wild noises grew more aggressive. Red bounced from his fur and filled the air around him. He tilted forward and pushed the bird downwards towards the clearing. Down the bird and Ebert flew.

Spiraling.

Spinning.

Gaining speed towards the Trebors below.

Chaos broke out once again. Trebors ran in all directions. All of them, except Yama, Yapa, and Elder Malc. They stood still, arms remaining stretched above their heads. Just as the bird was about to collide with the crowd below, it again pulled up its head and flew straight over them. But this time, Ebert jumped onto the ground from its back and crouched low at the edge of the clearing. The bird floated over him as he stood underneath it, lurking in its shadow.

Trebors everywhere froze and stared. Yama ran towards Ebert with her arms opened wide. Stella could tell she was yelling, but she couldn't hear anything that she said. Ebert bounced on his legs, up and down, and then crouched low again. Other Trebors moved slowly towards him as Yama ran. Yapa followed quickly behind. He joined Yama and together they moved carefully towards Ebert.

Stella flew closer to the scene as her heart raced quicker than she'd ever felt it do before. That's when she saw it. It wasn't a bird that hung over Ebert. It wasn't a bird that had carried him on his back. It was hundreds of tiny malpeds all locked together with their suction feet. They hadn't morphed into a bird, like they had the giant malped years ago, they had just strung themselves together to look like one. Their feet linked together and their skin stretched to fill in the empty space. The stretching of their skin made the form of the bird. The bird shape looked just like the one Stella sat on, except unlike the real bird, there were no feathers or colors, just naked scales shimmering as they hovered above the Trebor's clearing. It was grotesque.

Yama and Yapa were within a few feet of Ebert now. Ebert jerked back and wailed. He waved his arms around hysterically until without warning the shape of the malped bird exploded. Hundreds of malpeds burst from the shape and scattered onto the ground. They scrambled, climbed, slithered and ran throughout the clearing. Trebors screamed and ran for the tree's opening. Yama and Yapa turned from Ebert and ran to help the others. They grabbed young children and tucked them under their arms, throwing themselves towards the tree. Ebert jumped up and down again and cackled. Now Stella could hear, she could hear the piercing sound of her brother's laugh. *Not my brother*, she thought, *this isn't my brother anymore.*

"Faster," she screamed at the bird.

Ebert ran towards the tree now too. He jumped and threw himself at the tree, grasping the bark with his claws. Malpeds joined him on the tree, slinking around him. Some floated in the air around him and others stuck to the tree and climbed along with him. Ebert reached hand over hand, climbing quickly up the outside of the tree. He laughed as he climbed, throwing his head back so that the noise of his hysteria rose to meet Stella's ears with crystal clear sound. It tore at her ears and sent a thunderbolt of pain into her head. Now other Trebors climbed behind Ebert, yelling at him to stop. Yapa was among them, struggling to keep up with his son. Stella watched and felt so helpless. Until, all at once, she realized what Ebert was climbing for. She suddenly knew why he came back.

*The seeds.*

Once the sprigs of spring, like the evershi, begin to rise from the ground, the tree also pushes new life into its branches, which meant seeds were plentiful along the tree's branches. These seeds are immensely powerful. And now Ebert wanted them, or the malpeds wanted them. Either way, Stella knew that they would be used for evil, not for the goodness that the tree intends.

"Stop Ebert. Stop!" Stella tried again. This time she was close enough to be heard and Ebert jerked up his head and squinted into the sky. Quickly, he turned his face back to the malpeds and he cackled again. Yapa reached just below him and stretched his arm to grab Ebert's foot. He caught his heel, but Ebert shook him off violently. Yapa slipped off the tree and somersaulted through the air. Yama screamed.

One of the Trebors on the tree below Yapa moved with lightning speed to grab Yapa's shirt as he tumbled past. He caught him, threw him back to the tree, and Yapa safely grasped onto the bark with his claws. Ebert sneered and climbed even more rapidly as if gliding up the tree. The malpeds surrounded Yapa and kept him from moving any further. In fact, these tiny creatures blocked all of the climbing Trebors. Their red eyes glowed with intensity as they made a wall between Ebert and his real tribe.

The Trebors yelled together for Ebert to stop, with Yapa's voice ringing louder than all of the others. Ebert did not stop though, he just kept bounding up the tree, cackling and shaking as he went. When he finally did stop, he glanced below him and stared at Yapa. For a moment, Stella thought he might turn around, but then he reached out his hand to grab a seed sack that grew on one of the branches. Stella was now a few feet of the tree. She was almost within reach of Ebert.

She screamed again, "Ebert, stop. Look at me!"

Ebert clamped his hand around the seeds and laughed again. Stella grabbed at her heart as it lurched in her chest.

"NO!" she hollered.

Ebert bounced up and down on the tree branch. He waved the hand with the seeds in it and laughed harder. He was wild and no longer even seemed to notice the Trebors yelling from below. At his feet, green sparks flickered and shot into his claws as they gripped into the bark. Ebert hopped on one foot and then the other. He jumped up and down and looked at the branch below him. The tree was pushing its power into Ebert, rushing in to flush out the evil. The glowing red of Ebert's feet now flashed with green. As he bounced from one foot to the other the colors mixed. Ebert screamed as the two forces raged in him.

Stella yelled again, "Hold onto the tree!"

As she yelled, the bird, with Stella on its back still, swung its body around the tree and tilted so that Stella could reach for Ebert. Her hand grazed his back and she grasped at Ebert's overalls and fur. She missed. Ebert turned and scowled at the bird, and then at Stella, as they looped back around the tree. He jumped up and down and screamed louder. The sound was like the crackle of a fire. Green and red flew from his feet. Just as Stella was about to swing past Ebert again, just as she was about to reach him, he jumped.

He just leaped straight into the sky. Spirals of green chased after him into the air. Red streaks reflected against them. All the colors collided, exploded, and disappeared in the air above Ebert as he fell.

"NO," Yama yelled from the ground.

"Catch him," Elder Malc responded.

# CHAPTER 28

Trebors ran underneath where Ebert dropped. They opened their arms and braced themselves for the impact of his fall. Like the icicle in Stella's dream, Ebert's body gained speed as it pointed towards the ground; a spear heading towards the Trebors below. The malpeds that had been blocking Yapa and the others now jumped from the tree to follow Ebert.

The malpeds that had been on the ground in the clearing also leaped into the sky and spread their arms like wings. The malpeds gathered quickly in the space below Ebert. Their hundreds of feet suctioned together and their skin stretched to fill in around their bodies and further connect them. Instantly, they took on the shape of a bird again. The monstrosity spread its wings and raced towards Ebert. It caught him on its back seconds before he would have reached the ground and the arms of the Trebors below. It swooped into the sky. Ebert jerked on its back and jabbed his fist in the air. Stella could not see if he held the seeds, but she feared he still held onto what he came for. Abruptly, he turned his attention to Stella and the bird.

"Watch out!" Snu yelled from below, and he waved his arms over his head to get Stella's attention. "He's coming for you…"

Stella realized then that Ebert was flying toward her at increasing speed.

"Watch," she screamed at the bird.

The bird laid its head down low and caught the current of the wind blowing up and around the tree. It glided away from Ebert, but Ebert was not deterred. His snicker caught on the tails of the wind that propelled Stella and the bird, and the noise once again settled in Stella's chest and head. She held on more tightly to the feathers of the bird so she once again wouldn't fall off as they raced to keep away from Ebert.

Ebert flew alongside Stella and they focused on each other. She couldn't look away from the red that glazed over his once beautiful, blue eyes. He did not smile or cackle, he just burrowed his eyes into Stella's as if something were about to happen. She felt another chill drive up her spine and she tore her eyes away from him and rubbed them in one swift motion.

"Ebert, this isn't you. Stop!" she yelled.

Ebert did not reply but instead stood on top of the flying malpeds. He wobbled as he tried to find his balance. From below, Trebors screamed, no one more than Yama, whose pain flew to Stella's ears.

"Don't! You'll fall!" Stella tried again.

Slowly, Ebert shifted his feet, bit by bit, until he was standing sideways as he hurtled through the sky. His whole body faced Stella and the bird. He bent his knees and throttled himself towards her. Before Stella could respond, the bird lurched away sharply. Ebert's hands grazed the bird's feathers as he slipped through the sky. As he fell, he grabbed onto a small branch from the tree and it bounced as it supported his weight and stopped his fall. The malpeds in their bird shape swooped in to pick up Ebert, but he motioned for them to leave him and pointed at Stella.

The malpeds came towards Stella and this time were able to reach her before she and the bird were able to gain momentum to escape. They flew straight at her and then just when it seemed they would collide, the shape exploded as it had before. Hundreds of malpeds filled the sky and flung themselves towards the bird. They landed on the bird's head and all along its wings, they landed on its back and clung to its talons. Stella swung her hands with her claws out to try and push them off.

The smell that gathered around her made her feel sick and light-headed. She swiped at the malpeds even harder. She screamed. Trebors below did the same. Stella gasped for air as she tried to fight off the malpeds and the sound of their hissing drove pain deep into Stella's forehead. Her vision blurred and she had to stop fighting to regain her balance and strength. The bird lurched again. It fluffed its feathers around where Stella sat and the pain stopped instantly. Stella began swinging at the malpeds again.

"Help!" she bellowed.

The bird dropped a few feet and then bounced up again. Stella squeezed her legs tightly against its back to hold on as she fought. Then she realized, the malpeds were unable to attach to the bird. One by one they tried to suction to the bird, tried to get to Stella, but slipped off with every attempt.

Their feet moved quickly to hold onto the feathers, but they couldn't get a grip. The bird was repelling them; somehow the malpeds couldn't stick to it. Like raindrops, the malpeds plopped from the bird's body. Then the bird sent a quiver that started with its head and moved through to the tips of its wings, and in this one motion, any of the remaining malpeds flung from its body.

From below, cheers went up from the other Trebors. All along the tree, Trebors now climbed again to reach Ebert as he dangled. The malpeds regrouped in the air and immediately turned back into the shape of a bird. They did not set their sights on Stella this time but flew quickly towards Ebert. They skimmed his feet and he jumped on board. This time he looked differently though, he was less wild, and no longer threw off a red glow from his fur. From where he had been holding onto the tree branch, green radiated along his fingers down his forearms. Before Ebert could make any motion or get settled, the malpeds dove back toward Stella. Ebert jolted and quickly reached to grab the backs of the malpeds. In a flash, the seeds he clutched slipped out of his hand. They spun into the air and then dropped toward the ground.

"Get them!" Stella screamed to the bird.

"We have to catch them," another yelled from the ground.

The great bird and Stella soared toward the falling seeds. It flew under them and then snatched them in its beak. Narrowly missing the ground below, the bird swooped back into the sky. By now, the malpeds were fast behind the great bird. A high, piercing hiss radiated in the air around them.

The bird pushed its wing deeper up and down and gained more speed as it raced away from the malpeds. The malpeds gained, the force of their collective bodies in the shape of a bird gave them great strength and agility. Soon the malpeds were flying alongside Stella and the great bird.

The slightest whisper of the word "help" cut through the terrible hissing noise.

Stella snapped her head sharply towards where Ebert sat atop the flying malpeds. He did not look at her. He did not speak. He was limp and lifeless. All the wild had left him.

"Ebert, you've lost what you came for, you don't have the seeds. But you'll always have us. The tree will always save you. This can end now. Leave them. Leave the malpeds," Stella yelled.

Ebert began to shake and his fur stood on end all over his body. He closed his eyes and banged his forehead against the back of the malpeds and then jolted to attention and looked at Stella. His eyes had tears in them.

"Come back, we love you, we love you," Stella screamed.

"You still love me?" Ebert yelled.

"Always," Stella answered.

With that, Ebert began jerking around. He frantically wanted to get off the malpeds. Ebert tried to move his legs but they were suddenly suctioned to the malpeds. He motioned to lift his hand, but couldn't even pick it up. It was as if every part of him was glued to the malpeds. He pulled and pushed, his motions more frantic each moment. One of the malpeds slithered out from the shape of the bird and crawled up Ebert's back. Ebert instantaneously slowed and stopped trying to pull away his hands and legs.

"Help," came a muffled cry from Ebert.

"We have to do something, he wants help," Stella cried.

The great bird swung quickly away from the malpeds and Ebert. It then rode on the current to redirect itself toward Ebert. It carefully tilted its body until its wing pointed over Ebert's head. It swept past Ebert, brushing its feathers across his forehead. Again, the bird circled and came around, its wing tipped towards Ebert, Stella gripped on tightly as they swooped. Just as the tip of the wing feathers grazed Ebert, he reached up and grabbed on.

The bird jerked up to pull him. Stella lost hold and slid along its back. She just managed to grip onto the feathers before falling off. She hung off its tail feathers as it yanked upward with the weight of Ebert's pull. Finally, Ebert yanked free from the malpeds. His body catapulted off the backs of the malpeds. But he lost his grip on the bird's wing. The bird bounced up as Ebert flung free and lost hold. Stella flew from the bird's feathers and landed back on top of its neck. She held on with all her might as the bird dove towards Ebert. It reached him before the malpeds did and opened its beak to grab onto his fur and save him. The seeds. The bird dropped the seeds to save Ebert. Once again, the seeds rained through the air. Stella clambered onto the bird's head to reach for Ebert. The bird steadied its flight for her to get hold. She pulled him over the bird's beak and safely onto its head.

"The seeds. The seeds!" Snu yelled.

It was too late, the malpeds swooped down and grabbed

them. Every single one.

From her perch on the bird, with Ebert finally with her, Stella watched as the malped bird broke back into hundreds of tiny malpeds. They spread into the sky. There was no way of knowing which ones had the seeds. They scattered and flew away in all directions. Like a storm of locust, the malpeds darkened the sky as hundreds of them scattered away on the horizon. The hissing and putrid smell left with them. They disappeared from sight within minutes. Disappeared with the seeds. The sky silenced.

"Never again!" Ebert yelled. His voiced echoed around them, "I CHOOSE HOME!"

Green spirals shot from the tree's branches and landed on Ebert. The space around him glowed and a fresh, leafy smell bathed the air. The streaks of color whirled around Ebert as he sat on the bird.

Stella felt both joy and fear climb through her heart. The two so closely linked that she felt frozen as she sat next to Ebert on the bird's back. Ebert was back, but they had lost the seeds.

Ebert turned to his sister. "I'm sorry," he said.

Wind swept past them and the bird pushed its wings down hard to stay hoovering over the clearing. Stella looked towards Mt. Bor to see if she could get a glimpse of the malpeds. They had the seeds. They had to be stopped. She felt so angry with her brother, while also filled with relief that he was with her. She was speechless.

Ebert put his hand on his sister's shoulder as he spoke further, "I chose home, Stel. I want to be with the tribe, and I will work to make things right again. We will find the malpeds and we will get those seeds back."

"Are you really here to stay? Are you done with the malpeds and their tricks?" Stella asked.

"I know it might be hard to believe me now, but I am here to stay. I felt the tree's power surge through my body as it fought to save me. I felt the pull of the malpeds as they worked against the tree's power. But once my heart saw the truth, and I chose the tree and the tribe, I felt the malpeds' grip on me loosen. And then as the bird's wing tips brush over me it was like my body couldn't be held by them anymore. I was set free. That's when I grabbed the bird's wings. Do you see Stella, I understand now, I had to want to be with the tree, with the bird, with you, and our tribe!"

Stella almost couldn't believe the words that Ebert spoke. They felt too good to be true. But she saw in his face that he meant them. And she recognized in herself that all she could do was trust him and stop trying to control it all for him.

"I thought I could save you. But I see now. You had to want to be home. You had to choose us and our life with the tree. It never mattered how badly I wanted that for you, you had to want it for yourself."

Ebert nodded. They both knew that no matter how much they loved each other, they each had to own their own lives and had to make their own decisions. And in that moment, they both chose to do that together. They fell into each other's arms and suddenly they were bathed in the glow of the green from the tree. Stella clung to her brother and whispered, "Welcome home Ebert, welcome home."

# CHAPTER 29

Stella bolted upright and squinted to see the space around her. She put her hand over her heart and took a deep breath. Ebert slept soundly on his sleeping mat near-by. He was curled in a tight circle and snoring loudly. They had both collapsed into bed the night before and she felt relieved that she had gotten some sleep. The previous day now felt like both a magical dream that brought Ebert back to them, and a confusing nightmare that she couldn't quite make sense of.

While still sitting on the bird, Stella and Ebert had both been convinced that they needed to know where the malpeds took the seeds and what they did with them.

"We have to follow them," she had yelled to the tribe below them.

"Go!" Elder Malc had yelled back.

"I'm sorry all," Ebert had called to the tribe below.

"We forgive you," they had replied in unison as the bird began to fly.

All at once, the great bird had flown with speeds that Stella had never known before. It took them quickly over the Or Forest to the field at the foot of Mt. Bor where Stella had seen the stony pile of the giant malped's body earlier that day. They had circled the old trunk and flown all over the area looking for signs of the malpeds. They had found nothing.

Eventually, the two had realized there was nothing more for them to do, and asked the bird to carry them home. But it was as they did their final circle over the dead field and the foothills of Mt. Bor that they had noticed something new. Tiny green spots dotted the field. They glowed and sparkled despite the darkness and fog that carpeted the field and body of the giant malped. Ebert and Stella had turned to look at each other with horror. They didn't need to name what they saw. They knew what they were looking at and it had filled them both with dread.

Now, as Stella sat on her sleeping mat, watching her brother sleep, she shook her head to brush away the fear she had felt when she realized the seeds had been scattered in that field. At the base of the old trunk, and the feet of the pile of rubble that was once the giant malped, the great tree's green seeds had been sown. *Would they actually grow there? Could the trebors harvest the seeds and bring them back? Or would they be protected by the malpeds and untouchable? What happens when they grow amongst so much evil?* Stella wondered. Her head throbbed and she slowly lay back down on her mat. She felt a fresh wave of panic wash over her as she thought about the days ahead and the consequences of what they had seen. *Was it possible to have more than one great tree?* She asked herself.

# EXCITING NEWS

## THE TREBOR TALES, BOOK 3
## COMING FALL 2021

THANK YOU FOR BEING A WONDERFUL READER!

FOLLOW ON SOCIAL MEDIA *(WITH YOUR PARENT'S PERMISSION)* TO STAY
UPDATE ON TREBOR TALES NEWS, UPCOMING EVENTS AND GIVEAWAYS

INSTAGRAM @TREBORTALES
INSTAGRAM @CAROLINECBARNEY
FACEBOOK @CAROLINEBARNEYAUTHOR

WHAT DO YOU THINK ABOUT THE TREBORS? THE MALPEDS?
WHO IS YOUR FAVORITE CHARACTER?
CAROLINE WOULD LOVE TO HEAR FROM YOU.

CAROLINEBARNEY.COM/CONTACT
OR EMAIL MEDIA@TOUCHPOINTPRESS.COM

OTHER BOOKS IN THE TREBOR TALES SERIES
The Trebors, Book 1

*Beware the Trebor who ventures far,*
*for the smalls of darkness gather there.*

Bori is ravaged, the earth scorched, homes destroyed. Stella longs for the days of peace, where Trebor's danced and sang, where her tree home held all she needed. Now devastation surrounds her and worse yet, her father is missing. He didn't make it home before the storm ripped through the land. The devastated forest calls Stella to journey into it, to look for her father, and face down whatever hides in its deep crevices. But a shifting shape of evil lurks nearby and threatens to destroy everything she knows and loves.

Made in the USA
Middletown, DE
31 January 2021